The Temporary Husband

The Infamous, crazy Fletcher...

GW01057597

CHAPTER 1

The silence of the tombs, Innocencia Lockwood mused, and took a quick glance at the door. On seeing that no one was coming, she slumped back on the chair and grimaced when the hard, unrelenting back didn't give her the room she sought in order to relax. As to be expected, the chair was stiff, rigid and uncompromising like the general.

He usually claimed he didn't like people who slouched because it revealed a sloppy attitude about them. How he managed to sit up straight for eight hours and more, was a miracle to Innu, since in only an hour, both her butt and back ached.

She dragged out a weary sigh, uncrossed her long legs and crossed them again, exchanging which leg now remained above the other, then reached for the delicate china tea cup and took a sip of the tea.

Blah, it was now cold.

The sound of footsteps on the marbled floor had her ears perking up as Harty came into the room. Harriet Adams was an old, kind woman who'd been the family maid ever since Innu could remember. Innu has always called her Harty, since as a child she failed to pronounce her name due to the stammers that would overcome her at times, whenever she became overly excited or distressed. So the shorter version to Harriet's name stuck.

As usual Harty was beaming from ear to ear without a care in the world. She was one of those oldies who'd lived a full life and didn't appear to have a smidgen of guilt over the decisions she might have made in her youth.

"The general will see you now," Harty informed her and Innu audibly sighed like one resigned to her fate. Harty giggled at her exaggerated sigh.

"How is he by the way?"

"How do you think he is?"

Innu flicked her finger and excitedly replied, "Mellow." She then frowned at Harty's raised brow and twinkle in the eyes before she scratched her chin and vigorously shook her head, "Nope, no-no-no, that'll be a lie, there's never a time when I've seen him in that mood. He's anticipating how he'll make me suffer with that evil grin on the side."

"Silly girl," Harty huffed and pinched both of Innu's cheeks. "Go on and don't get him overly excited."

Innu stood akimbo and raised her brows, "I can't believe you said that. Am I that terrible? No that's beside the point, don't you think you got this all wrong. I'm the one most likely to get overly excited and get a heart attack."

The old woman waved her off, "Young lady go now, or do you want to wait for two more hours while you dawdle here with me once he gets started on those conference calls. I could surely use your hand in the kitchen."

"Harty," Innu gasped and Harty winked at her. Harty was right, if she didn't hurry, she was bound to wait for two more hours and she couldn't afford that. She resignedly removed her hands from her waist and childishly stuck out her tongue before she reached out to the bag on the other chair and walked out of the room, Harty's heartfelt giggles following behind her.

Once the general got started on his calls, there would be no end to them in sight. The man was a workaholic to a fault, despite having underlings to do his bidding. Where was Dwayne by the way? Wasn't he meant to keep her father from being busy? Wasn't that the reason he was stuck with Mia? So he remained at the helm of Lockwood's

Surveillance and Security firm, rather than branch out and live his life like the rest of them.

She huffed, as her mind went back to the problem at hand. One month is all she had, before Jane Cooper pulled the rug from under her feet?

Getting into the corridor, the neutral colors and cool undertones made the huge house seem more like a mausoleum than anything else. Innu inhaled and exhaled deeply, calming her already terse nerves.

God, how she hated coming back home. If it were up to her, she wouldn't be walking down this corridor, especially after the brave words she threw at her father a year ago. The general wasn't playing fair as far as she was concerned. First, he commanded her to come back to the city. Fair enough, she'd been away from home for a long time and it was understandable that after the corona pandemic, families wanted to remain in closer contact with each other. She took up residence in one of her mother's apartments, which could have been legally hers if only she hadn't stupidly signed it over to the general in her quest for independence.

When the general heard about her little mishaps from Jeremy, her blabber mouth of a step brother, he insisted she move back to the family home.

Well that wasn't going to happen. She was an adult, not one to tuck in her tail, all because she was having a few social difficulties. With her refusal to abide by her old man's wishes, the general took things to another level. How could a man be so infuriatingly vindictive? The general always got what he wanted from his children, despite how they tried to fight back. What soon followed was a series of embarrassing efforts from a tyrannical father to keep his daughter safe.

Her dad didn't shy away from ordering a few of his henchmen from his surveillance company to discreetly keep an eye on her and follow her everywhere she went. The men were unscrupulous in the same manner her father was. To them discretion didn't count, since their presence was forever felt whenever she decided to pull down her hair, throw back her heels and have fun. No wonder she was a quivering mass of jagged terse nerves, since instead of helping her out of her predicament so she returned to the once carefree Innu everyone knew, she was resigned to a spurt of panic attacks, jitters over the so called men specie and not to forget, her once upon a time active sex life was moot.

To add salt to injury, her father went on further to squeeze her life force out of her when he took away her credit cards, froze her accounts, repossessed her cars and threw her out of the beautiful apartment. The security detail pulled back too when she was thrown out!

When other fathers were busy welcoming their prodigal sons and daughters into the family fold and at the same time letting them retain their privacy, her dad was not only wringing her out to the world to dry out and die in his quest to bring her crawling back home, he had also removed the kid gloves where she was concerned and was now playing dirty.

Lucky for her she had a good support structure of friends, willing to help her out in her time of need. From them she learnt to live below her means, barely actually, but nonetheless it was way better to the control her father sought to have over her.

Three taps are all it took before she heard him answer in his gruff voice for her to enter.

"General," she greeted with a slight nod of her head. As usual he sat on the black leather chair, behind the huge oak desk in the office. Looking intimidating on all accounts in his gray tailor made suit. She straightened her spine. This was a meeting of the highest order.

"Are you now ready to move back home?"

Innu scoffed. "Not a chance general, like I mentioned before, my word in my bond. I'm not coming back."

"Innu." He frowned over the spurt of rebelliousness she was still showing and taped his lean fingers on the table top, then motioned for her to begin. "Let's hear it, I gather you have a proposal you want to make."

Nothing new there, it was a do or die situation, so Innu gladly started setting up her laptop, relieved at the same time that the general wasn't pushing her over moving back home. After the connections were done, she straightened up and smiled to the one man audience in the room before she began.

Once upon a time, she'd thought her family was the odd one out when she remarked to her friends that, every time she needed funds, all she had to do was make a solid business plan which she would present to her father. It was only after she heard about Gregory Henderson; Margaret's brother in law and on how he took a gap year before going to varsity by presenting a business proposal to his grandfather, that she realized her family wasn't odd at all, but pretty much ordinary in their circles. Children negotiated over how they led their lives. Ugh, such a doozy.

A series of rapidly fired questions followed during and after the presentation which left her reeling while the general grinned in satisfaction. She slumped on the chair, her body feeling like one that had been dragged under by a haul truck. The general chuckled softly, appearing to be enjoying this more as she groveled for his assistance.

"This is good." He flipped through the proposal she'd handed to him prior, grunted here and there, while her tummy fluttered in nervousness.

She wrung her fingers and discovered that she couldn't sit still for long, as she waited for the hatchet to fall. Standing up on unsteady legs, she moved towards the window which showed the view to the immaculately cut green grass, the rows of roses, dappling here and there including a variety made up of daffodils and tulips in the garden. The fountain in the middle, of an angel with a harp in hand, spouting out water from the music notes, completed the landscape ahead of the path with flourish.

Tamed, calm and serene on all accounts, the garden was like the general seated on his leather chair and going through the proposal in silence. Poor him, unlike the air he gave out, including his surroundings, she just happened to be that out of place anomaly in his tranquil life.

A clearing of his throat made her turn to face him.

"I'm impressed." But he shook his head nevertheless, the frown that now marred his features saying much. "Unfortunately I can't help you out this time."

She walked back to the seat and sat down. A breath of air whooshed out of her mouth which she hadn't realized she was holding. "Why? May I ask? Does it have anything to do with my refusal to move back home?"

He shook his head. "No Innu, this is about you being a high risk."

"What do you mean a high risk?"

"Why are all banks not willing to give you a loan?"

"You."

The general barked out a laugh. "Me. How so sweetie?"

She scoffed at the endearment. The general could at times goof around and that is why she always failed to catch his shrewd nature until it was too late. He would deliver his ultimatums with that same disarming smile on his face like it was nothing but a joke.

"How am I the problem?" the general gently repeated the question.

"For some reason, my name and surname bandied together have every bank stamping *denied* on my proposal."

Not to forget the connections you have, who are willing to do such favors for you, that is why I think you're the culprit.

"And you think it's because of me?"

Innu vigorously nodded.

"Innu, you know nothing about keeping your finances in order and you expect to get assistance from any financial institution with the bad credit you have, not to forget the businesses you've opened and shut on a whim. The bank's refusal to give you a loan might be due to that, rather than your perception of the influence that I might have over this," the general mildly answered.

Innu shook her head; of course she'd known he would say that and not out rightly admit that he'd pulled a few strings to make her surrender.

"I get it that I've opened and shut a couple of businesses. But those businesses were a success, remember. Despite what you might think, I always managed to settle the loans too. It's just that I couldn't carry on doing what I considered to be not interesting for the rest of my life. Now, I am serious about this."

The general scoffed. His expression said it all. He had heard that explanation. Beside the fact that on the loan part, he was the one usually bailing her out. "That is another issue. You do not pick a business and toss it aside the moment you feel you're now bored with it."

"Ugh, this is going nowhere," she groaned. "The inheritance general at least I deserve that. I'll be turning thirty five in a few months. Can't you fast track it so I receive the lump sum now?" She cut in instead; too nervous to let her latest dream slip by, considering this one was deeply etched in her heart, unlike her former dreams.

The general stared at her like she had sprouted a couple of horns on her head when she uttered those words. Before he could reply, a slight knock was heard and her grandmother entered the room.

"Nana!"

Innu scrambled from her chair and nearly cursed. Seeing the general didn't bat an eyelid, she realized she had fallen into a trap.

"At least you remember who I am." The old woman put aside her cane and hugged her before she pinched her ears. This was so embarrassing, Innu thought, trying to wrestle her ear from the old woman's grip.

"What is this I am hearing about you wanting to get my daughter's money before you come of age?"

Innu gulped, wait a minute. Was she out there listening to her asking for that?

"It's not as you think nana, I've a good and solid business proposal." Her nana rolled her eyes in exasperation and let go of her ear then sat on the chair. "Like we haven't heard that before. Remember that little business venture in Italy, what happened to it?"

"What happened in Milan is not my fault nana." Innu rubbed her ear and her grandmother shook her head. "You cheated on Drew."

"You can't mix business with pleasure. What Drew did was wrong?" Innu reiterated.

Her father's jaw dropped open before he closed it shut and her grandmother on the side sniggered.

"Hopeless case is what she is. I don't think she even sees it." Then her nana went on to recite Innu's scandalous relationships she'd gone through so far.

Innu groaned. "That was me then, this is me now. Why are we bringing up my history all of a sudden?"

"Prove it."

" Sorry—what?"

Her grandmother stared at her before she nodded to the general and he handed her a sheaf of papers for her to read.

"If you're so different and you've truly changed, prove it. This is the original Will to your mother's estate. I never thought we would've to use it since she'd given your father the leeway to change it to how he thought fit—which he did when you turned eighteen. Apparently Adele knew you better than any of us, and what your father did, only set you on a path that none of us ever anticipated."

"What are you talking about grandma?" Already her mouth felt dry after reading the first statement on the will, written in her mom's beautiful elegant handwriting. She thought that she also caught a whiff of her subtle floral scent her mom used to wear, and Innu now also wore.

The further Innu read the will, the more her eyes widened. She went back to the lines before she retorted, "This can't be it."

A satisfied smirk graced her Nana's lips. "Like I said, prove it."

Innu slumped back on the chair in a daze.

No it can't be.

No, this was probably a huge joke or a terrifying nightmare which she wanted to get out from very fast. A pinch on her arm would wake her up.

The general grinned at the stunned wounded expression on her face and her grandmother remarked. "Guess you don't have an excuse then of living in the way you've been doing for some time now. Having the endless string of relationships and not setting roots"

"Nana!" Innu hissed and her grandmother had the audacity to shrug her shoulders, pretending like she wasn't aware of the struggle Innu was currently going through and over why she hadn't set any roots like she'd put it.

"Dad." She turned to face the general instead. "This project is important to me. I swear I will pay you back. At the same time I can't do this!" She flapped the papers in the air.

"Dad." A furrowed brow on the general's face and then he grinned. "Don't you think it's too late for you to start calling me that? Enough love. My hands are tied. I should've never tried to change the will in the first place , but seeing how you went about using up a quarter of your inheritance, has convinced me that your mom knew what she was doing."

Innu gulped down a few breaths. This couldn't be happening, considering this was her last resort.

She abruptly stood up from the chair and moved around the office like a caged animal. Jane Cooper's voice drifted in her thoughts, *One month is all I can give you or the building will be sold to another.*

She thought of June, Precious and Sweetie, girls she'd come to know in that short period of time, whom she'd come to count on as family. Girls who hadn't known better and were paying the ultimate prize.

"No, I can't." She vehemently shook her head in horror, at the thought of the contents in the will and watched in disbelief as her nana leaned in to address her former son in law.

"Settling down is the next best thing don't you think and it's about time too, she's been putting this away for far too long. I need great grandchildren to sit on my lap and pull my hair just like any of the grandmother's around. I want to be called nana of the year, and this girl has kept me from being that."

Children!

Innu clutched on her throat. Please not that. *Blood, too much blood,* she faintly thought. The sound of a child wailing feebly, echoed in her ears as a reminder of what shouldn't have happened if only...

She clutched her chest.

Not again, she thought, trying to stay calm. This couldn't be happening especially at this particular time when she had her life under control. *Everything is under control.* She inhaled deeply and slowly exhaled, the two adults speaking over her like she was no longer in the room.

Don't panic, she muttered beneath her breath. *There is nothing scary at all about this. This is for the girls. All I need is to get married and have a platonic relationship with the man.*

*What if he doesn't agree to all this, h*er mind mocked. *It's just a matter of time before he finds out, or they all find out what a fraud you are.*

HOW COULD I HAVE BEEN SO CARELESS? She flinched as the wailing increased.

No, think present, she furiously shook her head.

"One year can't be a hardship to start on those children," the general said.

The word children pierced her internals again.

"Children are a joy." Her granny added and the wailing continued. When did that simple conversation of getting married suddenly get to the part of children?

"Innu." Her dad frowned in alarm at noticing how pale her face had gotten as she thumped on her chest with her fist, her pacing having come to an abrupt stop.

"I can—I can't believe," she looked at her father and nana who now wore concerned expressions on their faces.

She'd never said anything to them. How could she, when she knew how deeply hurt they would be with her actions. It was better for them to think she was having a midlife crisis. That whatever she was going through could be sorted out with just the snap of their fingers and the damned will.

To prove her for the fraud that she was, instead of that thought keeping her sane, the guilt wrapped around her like a second skin, shame and grief following behind on its heels. The wails of a baby became louder no matter how hard she tried to ignore them, as the walls crowded her and the ceiling changed shades. The last words she heard was of her father saying her name, "Innu!" before she slumped on the floor in a faint.

"FOR SOME REASON I KNEW that wasn't going to end well," Jeremy said.

"Ooh shut up Jeremy. This is actually good for Innu," Dwayne retorted.

"She wouldn't have fainted if this was good for her."

Innu slowly opened her eyes. She was in her room, laying on the bed, her two step brothers standing on opposite sides and talking over her. Yapping like hormonal soft men as they usually did whenever they met.

"Please go and fight somewhere else," she groggily let out, irritated as usual that people around her always managed to talk about her like she wasn't there. She slowly woke up from the bed. Jeremy rushed to assist her. She shook his hand off. He laughed at her reaction then greeted, "Welcome to the land of the living." Innu scowled at him. It was so typical of Jeremy to pretend like he cared, when they both knew that he was mommies favorite and no good thing ever came from that.

She warily looked at her older step brother, Dwayne. Broody as usual, taking everything in slowly like he had all the time in the world to say his piece.

"What are you both doing here at ho-home?"

Jeremy handed her a glass of water after she choked on the last word. He chuckled easily like the fish wife he probably was, when she glared at him, before she reluctantly took the proffered glass and took a sip from it.

"I just thought of dropping by after dad hinted that you will be going under the cane like Dwayne here."

Jeremy has always addressed his step father as dad, unlike Innu and Dwayne who called him general. When Jeremy's dad passed, he was only three years old and couldn't remember how he looked, so calling the general 'dad' came easily to him unlike to Dwayne who at that time was fifteen.

"And you thought why not, let me dash home and gloat over all this. Poor Innu being put under the cane like Dwayne."

Jeremy frowned. "No big sis, I just wanted to be here for you. I mean it must be hard as it is considering—," he never finished because Dwayne had moved to his side so fast before he could do so, shoved at him and yelled, "OUT!"

Jeremy looked in disbelief at his older brother then Innu. Whatever expression he might have seen on Innu is the one that caused him to storm out of the room and bang the door after him. Dwayne walked towards the bed, gingerly sat on it like any moment he would dash out if Innu decided to get violent and scratch his face up.

"I'm sorry about that."

Innu huffed and turned her face to the wall. "You should have kept quiet over my little mishap you know. Now everyone knows and then there is this thing about the will."

Dwayne slowly smiled. "The will has nothing to do with your little mishap and you know it. Whether you like it or not, it was written down way before."

Innu scowled. Dwayne said that like it would get him off the hook.

"Oh by the way, how's Mia doing," she asked instead, just to goad him too like he usually managed to goad her. The smile on his face was quickly wiped out like it hadn't been there. She could literally feel the atmosphere in the room sapping out of all the energy and getting cold, the tension palpable to the point one would use a knife to cut through it and she also had a feeling that icicles hung above her head, ready to fall on her face, fleecing it to mince meat if she were to say something that would piss Dwayne off. Just too much water had gone under the bridge where they were both concerned, with Mia being at the center of it.

"Mia is fine," her step brother coldly answered with a hint of threat in his voice, that said it loud and clear, this was a no go area and she knew it.

Dwayne stood up from the bed and tugged at his tie. "I should get going since your little fainting episode in the study was just that, a false alarm."

"I'm sorry I didn't live up to your expectations and die so you got my inheritance too."

"Innu," Dwayne growled. "I'm not your enemy here."

"Yah right, says daddy's golden boy or should I address you as daddy's golden retriever since when he orders you to go fetch, you do it gladly and in a hurry."

Dwayne looked at her with a frown, like one used to her sharp barbs and no longer could be riled up over them. "You know what, if I was the evil villain in your life that you make me out to be, I would've left you that morning and not been with you afterwards when you dealt with the—"

"I HATE YOU just go away," Innu screamed and flung a pillow at him. He dodged it. His face broke into that sexy irresistible smile, which usually had women tripping over their feet to get another look at him.

"No sweetheart, you do not hate me. You hate yourself for being vulnerable around me. I do know you remember."

She gasped at the lazy way he ran his eyes over her body, before she reached for another pillow. He ducked as it sailed past him.

"OUT!" Innu screeched.

Dwayne chuckled and lazily retreated to the door, walking backwards in case she decided to pick something heavier than a pillow and throw it at him. Innu was panting heavily and glaring his way.

"One question little sis." He ground out *the little sis part* like it was an unpalatable dish to chew at. "If you were so kind enough to call me a pimp when I got engaged, what should I address you as, seeing you're now boxed on all sides in the situation that I found myself in three years back? If you were to get married in order to keep your inheritance, what would that make you out into—a prostitute? I mean you do realize you will be selling yourself like one hmm." He sniggered; shut the door behind him as another pillow hit against it. Innu hollered a few nasty words about his character, slumped back on the bed before she cradled her face and wept.

CHAPTER 2

Innu pushed the luggage trolley forward, at the same time frantically looking for a way of escape. "Hey Innu, what's the rush?" Giles asked when he caught up with her and she nearly groaned in frustration. He placed his suitcase on the already full trolley. How she longed to precariously balance the trolley so it fell on the floor, while she dashed away from him as quickly as possible. She took in a few quick breaths and pulled on a smile. "Busy, busy Giles, that's why the rush."

She pushed the trolley and his hand on her shoulder made her abruptly stop. "I know you are busy darling, but I was thinking, you come over to our usual spot at the hotel after the wedding. For old time's sake hey."

Innu clutched hard on the handle. How of all people could she bump into him on her flight to Harmony? To top it all, she was forced to make small talk with him, when all she wanted was to lie back and think of her dilemma at hand. He was nothing but a guy she once had fun with and currently she was running away from those.

During the flight, she gave him a couple of hints to show that she wasn't interested, like the one worded answers to his questions, lying back on the seat and plugging earphones in her ears, which he plucked out. She opened a novel, pretending to be interested in it, a latest thriller by Crescentville's bestseller author Y. A Leone, only to have it removed from her lap and for Giles to narrate what happens next. Great. It's either he was too thick headed or he just chose to ignore the blatant and certainly clear, undisputable hints.

"I'm sorry Giles, buuut I can't. I have other commitments after the wedding. I'm sure your wife and kids look forward to having more of you around."

He sniggered. "Since when did you become modest? You never cared that I was married before. Are you trying to play hard to get?"

Innu briefly shut her eyes and slowly opened them, in the hopes he would have vanished from her sight by then. "It's because you conveniently forgot to inform me of that fact when we first hooked up!"

"Tell me, when would that have happened darling, hmm. When your hand was in my crouch and you whispered that I join you in the room, or better yet, when we were blatantly making out on the dance floor. Fun is what I was out for and you were game, so don't act the injured party here."

Yah right, she got it. She was terrible and always fell hard for these handsome tall glasses of wine, who would conveniently at the drop of a hat, hide their wedding rings and go out to clubs when they should be reading bedtime stories to their children.

Gosh, this was crazy, including the fact that this confrontation was about to make her shriek out in a panic, if he continued with his unrelenting pursuit of her.

"People change. I don't have that fun bone anymore."

He incredulously looked at her. Then a lazy grin spread on his handsome face as he ran his eyes over her body. She felt like sticking needles into his eyes. Not only did he make her feel dirty by that appraisal, her skin felt like tiny ants were crawling on it. He was just coming on too heavy. Why hadn't she noticed that before? The last time she'd heard anything about him, was that he'd divorced and married a third wife. His secretary. Guess that was going on a lot, considering her step brother married his secretary too.

"Come on baby. It will be fun." He drew closer to her and pushed her hair from her face,then straightened her dark tinted glasses, running his fingers lightly on her face. She sharply inhaled, which to him might have sounded like her usual *baby touch me again thing*, except that sharp intake of breath had to do with her slowly losing it and wanting to get out of the airport as fast as she could.

She ground out her teeth and shifted away. "I said I am not interested." Her sharply said words made him narrow his eyes on her. Giles wasn't one to be easily intimidated.

"I mean—,"she fanned her hands on her face and dragged in more air before she exhaled softly. "Like I said. I'm busy, that-is-all."

"Huh."

"Ya." She pointedly eyed his suitcase and waited for him to retrieve it from the trolley before she pushed it away as fast as she could; heading towards her freedom in the hopes that Giles wouldn't realize that change was an understatement. It was more of a total transformation, from lioness to tortoise.

When she was coming out of the airport, she yelped at the hand that grabbed her, spun her around and kissed her. Everything in her rebelled at his touch and kiss, revolted beyond words as beads of sweat formed on her forehead and under the armpit, while she tried to wiggle herself from his arms. Giles proved to be a stronger foe, plunging his tongue into her mouth while she fought for air. Clawing her way as she possibly could before stunning everyone with her fainting episodes, she bit hard on his tongue and with her heeled sandal stamped on his foot.

"Bitch!" He swore. "Feisty as usual but I will get you for this," he yelled, after he had abruptly let her go.

She was now clutching onto the trolley trying to recover, at the same time relieved that there were a few people coming out and going into the airport, who appeared to be more interested in their affairs than her little drama playing out.

"I said I am not interested, who—who—," she stammered and shook her head to clear it up from the hazy feeling that had set in. "Who—gave—gave you the right to paw at me like that." Giles made like he wanted to draw close again, concerned now.

"Innu."

She grabbed her vanity case and looked at him with a threat in her eyes. "No Giles, stay away if you know what is good for you." He opened his mouth to say something, looked at her hands that were shaking and tightly holding onto the vanity case like her life depended on it.

A voice of a little girl yelling her name, made Innu turn to the parking lot where she spotted Marg and Lucy rushing towards her.

"We will talk when you are no longer this emotional," Giles said and she huffed as he walked away from her.

"Aunt Innu!" Lucy screamed again. Innu picked Lucy up when she reached her and swung her up her arms. Lucy squealed in delight as she was tossed into the air before she received a couple of smacking kisses on her chubby cheeks and was placed back on solid ground.

Innu was more than relieved to see her friend and her family, that little episode with Giles having shaken her more. She still could feel the tremors down her spine. Tossing Lucy into the air proved to be good for her, because by the time she turned to face her friend, she had regained a third of her confidence.

"Marg love," she screamed like a teen and hugged her.

She slid her dark tinted glasses over her forehead afterwards and watched the handsome man approaching them, with three year old Gail in his arms. The man could surely turn heads and he didn't have to try to be noticed in order to do so. Even though he wasn't dressed in those fancy Ethan Ross suits but rather had put on blue Calvin Klein faded jeans, Gucci polo shirt and dior black sneakers, gosh, no matter what Garret wore, he looked tasty for eating.

"Good God Marg, you still haven't left him after that scandal," Innu said and feigned a horrified expression on her face.

"Why would I leave my husband in his time of need? It's me, him and the kids in our case. All against the world."

Innu scoffed. "Kids my foot. It's the package beneath the sheets that you value more. Guess the sex is crazy and you just can't get enough of it despite him having been on that deep end."

"I heard that," Garret said.

Marg pinched her, while Innu looked unapologetic at Garret. "How are you Pastor Gee?" She smiled up at him, before Garret handed Gail to his wife and hugged her.

"Better than you. I have a great sex life with my life partner as you can tell from that afterglow she has on. How do you think you will duplicate this afterglow when you are not yet set on one partner?"

Innu gasped and hit his arm, she couldn't believe he'd actually said that. No scratch that, Garret has always been outspoken. He was one of those unique pastors who said their mind without fear on how the other party would receive it.

She giggled at Marg who was glaring at her husband, including hissing at him to not say such things in front of their kids.

"She started it," Garret pointed out. Marg rolled her eyes.

Marg handed Gail to her. Innu gladly cooed, "Look at how grown up you are now my little princess." She repeated the same stunt she had pulled out on Lucy, tossing Gail into the air. Gail squealed in delight.

Margaret's little princess is so cute, she thought.

"I said I'm sorry for giving Marg a plane ticket to leave you the eve of the wedding. I mean look at you," she motioned to his height and physique, then pointed to her friend's height and physique while she played with Gail. "I feared for Marg and the fact that she would not survive the wedding night with you. All that talk about you not having rights on her. The wedding signaled you would have those rights and was going to make my friend pay for all the time you had abstained from sex."

Garret laughed. "Innu, same as always. Tell me, does your mind ever venture out of thinking about sex?"

Well it has actually, for three years, not that you will believe it if I said it aloud.

"Not a bit, not a bit darling." Innu winked at him, and then continued to walk past them to the car with Gail in her arms since the little girl had refused to be put down.

She was animatedly chatting with Marg when Garret got into the car after he put away her luggage in the trunk.

He turned to face them. "Honey."

"Oh, don't worry love; I'll sit at the back so I can catch up with Innu."

"Honey," he slowly repeated again. Innu snarled. She wondered how he managed to ruffle her without raising a finger. "I am not going to pollute your wife Henderson. On second thoughts, Marg go and sit next to him, I'd rather talk to Lu and Gail."

"I just don't get you guys—." Marg resignedly got out from the backseat and shifted to the front. "You love each other, why don't you admit it than try to piss each other off at every turn."

Eeeuw, Innu snorted in disgust and to her shock it was in unison with Garret. Garret stared at her and they both laughed while Marg continued to chide them on their behavior. Gail tugged on her shirt. "What did you bring me?"

"Lots darling. We'll take a look in the treasure closet once we get home."

"What about me?" Lucy chirped in, tucking herself under her arm and producing that winsome Henderson grin. Lucy would surely be trouble and have Marg and Garret placing her in a fortified castle once she got into her teens. Both the girls actually, seeing Gail was also one of the cutie pies Aggy had used for her newest baby range.

"You too sweetie."

Margaret's precious little girls continued with their questioning while Innu humored them. An ache had already set in too. How could her mother request this of her? If only she'd known that by the time those terms were made clear to Innu she would be broken beyond repair, she would never have insisted upon it.

What she was doing now, could fill the void that she always felt. Would it assuage her guilt, she wondered. But at least it did give her a semblance of peace. Not this... Despair filled her up on that sad thought while her friend's girls animatedly chatted with her.

She must have dozed off, because the next moment, she was being woken up by Marg. They had arrived at the farm.

She looked outside to the huge farm house and opened the door. Gail was soundly sleeping in her arms and she quickly handed her to the nanny who rushed out to them. The nanny took Lucy too, who was now sleeping on the seat.

"Wow, this is nice." She appreciatively looked around at the beautiful place, then she deeply inhaled the clean fresh air. Two men retrieved her luggage out of the trunk as Garret came around to her side.

"You like," Garret asked her.

"Henderson, how many children had you anticipated when you built this place?"

"Guess all you want," he answered with a grin, before he walked away from them.

"It's been thirteen years and this place always manages to make me stand in awe."

"Come on, let's get you freshened up and rest." Her friend said before she pulled her into the house.

"I can't believe you have been married to bloody Henderson for that long," Innu commented once they were in the huge, luxurious guest bedroom which contended with the Imperial hotel. Marg liked her comfort including providing the same for her guests. Innu retrieved the glossy wrapped gift from her bag and handed it to Marg.

"What is it?" Marg's excitement as usual was infectious as Innu watched her shake the box. Innu giggled at how Marg acted like her daughters. Two pony tails on her head and Marg would be back to being a teenager again. She hadn't aged at all.

"I don't know, open it when you are alone, I repeat—alone."

"These are for the girls." Innu continued and removed more packages.

"Innu you shouldn't have."

"I know—I know, your husband is monied and my budget is a bit tight of late, but let me have the pleasure too of seeing the beautiful smiles on the girls faces. This is for Garret."

Marg widened her eyes, "You got something for Garret?"

"Yes, why not? true to his word, he has been good to you."

Innu frowned when Marg reached for her phone and demanded, "Say that again. I need to record this for him."

Innu shook her head, Marg was still a clown. She then spoke loudly over Marg's phone which was in her hand. "Henderson, you've been true to your word, so I bought you a little something as an appreciation for being so good to my friend....happy now?" she asked Marg after.

"Innu are you dying," the deep voice came from the other end of the line to her shock. No, her friend didn't. Innu squealed in mortification and tried to grapple the phone from Marg. Apparently instead of recording a voice note, Marg had called her husband. She gave up on trying to wrestle the phone from Marg and walked further away from her.

"Are you not going to say more?" Garret's voice still drifted to where she stood.

"More—on what."

"Remember our bet." Of all things, the horrible man hadn't forgotten about it. Besides they were three years late and she had other pressing issues than the silly bet they made a long, long time ago.

"Marg, just take the gifts and go, and as for you Henderson, your saving grace is my poor friend. She loves you so much to the point she thinks you will never do any wrong in her sight. If it wasn't for those rose tinted eyes of hers, you would have been in the same boat like me, faith or no faith. *Capisce.*" Garret snorted while Marg giggled and carried away the gifts after she hung up.

Innu sighed, and sat on the bed. She braided her hair into two cornrows before she tied the braids up with a band, so it didn't get wet.

You can do this, she mumbled beneath her breath, stood up from the bed while she stared at her image in the mirror.

Oh hell. Looking at her was one scared woman who was about to tackle something way over her head. A miracle is what she would need to pull off this feat. That is, if she didn't manage to finally die from her panic attacks that would set in when least expected.

CHAPTER 3

"I still don't get why I have to do this," Bill grumbled and turned around to eight pairs of eyes critically assessing his appearance. Creepy is what they were.

"Cliff is your brother, that's why, and you are the oldest person in the family who is still yet to be leg shackled. You might never know, maybe his luck will rub onto you," Leonard said. Gifford walked up to him and dusted an imaginary fleck off his suit with a flick of his fingers. "You look great. Once the ladies notice you next to Cliff, they will drool and throw themselves your way."

"Yah, make sure during the introduction, you point out that the best man is single and he is about to reach the matured age of forty, fine wine has never tasted better," Gordon added and had his brothers in stitches over his expense, including his younger brother Edward who was now twenty one and according to their father, would be following down the marriage route in a few months time.

Bill hadn't noticed that time had flown by. *How could you when you have been moving in a daze,* his mind mocked.

It was unbelievable that almost all his step brothers had actually settled down. It was even more unbelievable that his womanizing twin brothers, the worst in the lot, had found themselves respectable women, who adored them wholeheartedly and didn't appear to be concerned over their unruly behavior, and if it were to be believed, they were now reformed.

"Guys you know me, ladies are no—," he never finished because Cliff walked out of the changing room and everyone's eyes shifted and focused on him.

Cliff grinned. He sure looked happy about his impending nuptials, unlike him who was being made the butt of a family joke. He snorted on that note, relieved at the same time that he was no longer the center focus.

He joined in the rowdy crew that was whistling at Cliff, made up of his brothers and friends. The groomsmen as it were usually put. A rowdy bunch too, testosterone going around in the room as everyone tried on the suits for the wedding and last minute adjustments were made. Cliff motioned to his suit and turned around, enjoying the pairs of eyes looking at him. "I've never felt this much expensive before, you really outdid yourself this time," Cliff said to the designer Ethan Ross, who sniggered in return. Bill rolled his eyes. Then for some reason everyone had an issue when he dressed up and coined a funny phrase about it. Look at them. He watched his brothers and Cliff's friends looking at themselves in the long length mirrors, and then asking each other how they looked.

"The ladies will not know what hit them," Max, one of Cliff's friends remarked and Bill scoffed. Now this guy loved women to the boot. If the ladies knew better, they would stay clear of his path.

No relations, his brother in law and former lover once advised, the day he visited Marg his little sister. His conscience had suddenly grown on him and he was becoming restless over his lifestyle, hence had gone to seek counsel from his shrink of a sister, but met her husband instead, the Spiritual counselor who unnerved him most of the time because of the radical transformation in his life.

And to think he had chosen the lesser evil between the two, figuring a radical life change isn't what he was searching for. Marg would comfort his soul and throw bits of platitudes to make him feel better about himself. Instead he found out when he got to the farm that Marg was at a sleepover at Sophie's place.

Garret asked him over what was going on with him, when he lingered in the living room after that little bit of unexpected news.

He was sitting on the couch, after having put his little girl, Lucy to bed. Different types of toys were strewn on the carpeted floor and one could have missed the floor due to that clatter since Lucy apparently was spoiled rotten by dotting parents who overwhelmed her with stuffed dolls including the ones that were larger than her body size.

The minister looked spent, in his opinion, wearing a gray t-shirt and faded jeans minus shoes on his feet, yet the smile he still wore on his face was of pure and utter contentment with his life.

Bill hesitated slightly and made up his mind fast. He sat on the other couch in the room, after shoving away the delicate tea set and the dolls that had been placed there, to enjoy the invisible tea and said his piece, or he whined over his lot in life, he couldn't remember the details except that he had felt caged then.

"Abstain, just for a year and see how it goes." That was the advice he received afterwards. Huh. He sat there on the couch stunned, while Garret seemed like he was enjoying this when he delivered his advice with flourish.

Of all the advice that he could give out, that was it. Why not tell him to go climb Mount Everest, better yet, go and look for the ruins of Babel.

"That's it, abstaining. You've got to be kidding me. I abstain all the time when I am not in a relationship. What is my abstaining going to solve?"

Garret shrugged his broad shoulders. "You just told me that you are feeling guilty every time you go the whole way in a relationship. Sleepless nights have become the norm afterwards. You do not need rocket science to solve your issue. Just put away intimacy from the table, for a year if possible."

Bill looked at him in disbelief and abruptly stood up from the chair. This was useless. Already he knew something was off with Garret. He had heard of his unconventional solutions. And to think he'd actually given him the benefit of doubt. As it turned out, it was true. Garret

Henderson had played hard in the devil's field and now played hard in God's field. Both extremes in his way of thinking.

Abstaining!

What kind of bs was that? And for a freaking year if possible.

Extreme indeed.

Especially for a freaking Fletcher! Their libido was legendary. One didn't gain such a reputation by twiddling their thumbs up and going through one year without sex.

Garret, a Henderson in this case, even failed the one year with his little sister. They were married off in haste by his gramps. If it hadn't taken Marg a few years to conceive after the marriage, he would have thought the reason why Garret and Marg had that little family wedding before their huge wedding is because she was already knocked up.

He reached out to the door knob when Garret's deep voice drifted to him. "The more you try to shut down the voice by pursuing those kinds of relationships, the emptier you will feel. Keep that in mind, Bill. The one year I suggested was meant to give you clarity."

Bill's back stiffened. Well Garret had him right there at the corner, and so he reluctantly began his journey.

For a minute though, he did feel like telling Garret to shove his advice somewhere else, he would wait for his little sister to give him the proper advice that he sort. She understood what it meant to be a Fletcher. Better yet, he should have sought advice from his older brothers. Booze and more booze would have done the trick and not to forget, boxing, since that would have been their solution.

So, were the months of abstaining easy? Not in the slightest.

The first two months were complete torture, they weren't clarity at all in his mind except for torture in every possible way, in his mind and flesh. It was like a huge gate had been opened over in his life to show everything that he would miss out by doing it Garret's way.

The gay bars he used to frequent called out to him even more, and he could swear the withdrawal symptoms included an enticing voice in his head, purring seductively for him to enjoy the carnal delights of the flesh.

Then it got crazy. Men, including women who knew he was gay, started throwing themselves at him. Straight men and women, okay. How was that even possible?

If he had thought he was way better than his father Aaron Fletcher, could hold his own where that self control department was, he realized that he was as much a weak person as him because it did happen.

How could it not when he faced the same problem his forefathers had faced, beautiful women throwing themselves at them. It was like the devil had said, *okay Bill you said you no longer want men on the table, shall we start, women, here we go.*

Old gay Bill had scruples, while new Bill acted impulsively, did what came to mind and dealt with repercussions after. He reminded him of someone he once knew. Right, young Bill who had been buried deep inside of him, hiding away throughout the course of the years.

He lost control of his car, and probably the engine got ripped off in the process because he went to bed with one woman and woke up the next with another.

Elle was a trusted friend and air hostess. He was furious like a gander with her and what she insisted had happened the previous night. This felt like those horror films that had a loopy time travel thing going on, because he couldn't get out of it. Then it began to look more like a set-up, including the fact that Garret had pointed out to him prior that his self effort wouldn't help him, not even by a mile. Total surrender to his Maker was key.

"Geez can't you get your shit together to make it up to your room," he swore, after he got into the living room and found the so-called cunning minister in the hot embrace of his wife, in their living room.

Marg yelped while Garret laughed. Bill had averted his gaze and turned his back on them.

"You are in our house. Whether we feel like having it out there on the porch, how does that concern you? If your head wasn't stuck in the ground as usual, you would have realized that no one was around the premises, or made a call before you came over for a visit."

Bill grimaced. Of course he had noticed that fact, but was intent on getting to Henderson and punching him if need be for daring him to abstain for a freaking year. His advice had opened up a can of worms.

"Go on up honey, I'll join you in bed in a few minutes." A sound of the rustle of clothes could be heard, zippers being dragged into place punctuated by giggles from his sister and kissing sounds. Good grief, couldn't these two keep their hands off each other for long enough to attend to his problem.

"Nice to see you Bill," Marg happily hollered at him and he flinched. She surely had the energy of a three year old despite now being a mother of two. By the way was she even meant to be undertaking such activities considering she had recently given birth?

Didn't women wait for three months to be given the all clear? He could swear for three months Leo was a grouch after his wife gave birth and as to be expected, his brothers got the brunt of it. Their boxing matches had turned deadly during that period.

Bill's eyes fell on the couch in the corner of the huge living room. Garret's jacket was carelessly draped on it, including his tie and Marg's clutch purse and baby pink silk scarf. Guess the two had come in from a date, and what he had interrupted had been about to get down in that living room.

"This has better be good Bill or I will cut your balls for the interruption." Garret brushed past him, buttoning up his shirt and heading back into the corridor.

"Charming as always", Bill mumbled beneath his breath and sauntered to the study after him.

He watched Garret pour two glasses of scotch after he sat down, studied the man beneath his lashes at how easily he walked in his home and his masculinity evident for all to see. Broad shoulders, tempered narrow waist and snug fitting slacks over strong lean legs. Garret still kept an active lifestyle, and the callused warm hands, evidence enough that even though he was a pastor to a mega church, manual labor wasn't alien to him in the least. Garret handed the glass to him and sat on the chair.

"What is it, what's wrong?"

"I'm beginning to think you are the devil's advocate. That is what's wrong."

A dark raised brow from the infuriating handsome man followed before he asked. "Why would you say that?"

"Okay, I admit, I can't do it. Happy now."

Garret chuckled softly and took a sip of his drink. Bill did the same, a bit disquieted at the fact that, where once upon a time he had been attracted to the boy he once knew; in his place was a man who didn't stir him in the least.

"I am not happy Bill because you have failed. What I'm happy about is that instead of trying to rely on yourself, you can now start to depend on the one who is dependable and who has been looking forward to meeting you for a long time."

Bill snorted. "There you go again, being all preachy."

"Like I said Bill, there is no other way except His." Henderson produced the bible from his drawer and hesitated to hand it over to him.

"One quick question, what brought about your little budging in episode into my home when yesterday night you were quick to tell me over the phone to go screw myself after I told you I sensed something wasn't right?"

Bill swore. "Did you set me up? Is that it?"

Garret narrowed his eyes on him. "You still haven't answered my question. For your information, I was here and you were a thousand and so kilometers away in a different city. As underhanded at times as you think I do things to make someone realize the truth. I never play dirty. That's the devil's forte."

Bill opened his mouth to refute, hesitated and snapped it shut. This was all on him, including the bruises and cuts he had borne on his body, and not forgetting the scene Ella had caused.

"I figure everything did go wrong with you then."

Garret was watching him, studying him like he was an alien who had just landed in his home. Bill nodded.

Garret grinned. "So what happened?"

"I don't want to talk about it."

Unlike his sister who would have prodded until she came to the truth, Garret merely nodded and continued to hand him the bible.

"Henderson what am I meant to do with this". He asked in exasperation. Garret shrugged his shoulders and stood up from his chair.

Bill turned the heavy bible in his hand in confusion.

"Read it, or better yet like a child, get down on your knees and holler, HELP to your Heavenly Father. Now I should go and finish what my beautiful woman and I had started."

That was it. His whole confused life summed up in just one little word, HELP.

Bill rolled his eyes as he watched his brother in law rush out of that study like one who had been just humoring him by trying to listen to his problem, when in actual fact, he was thinking about the delectable woman in his bed.

Crazy, Bill had thought, before he resignedly stood up from that chair and got out from the huge farmhouse.

He now realized why his conscience had suddenly awakened and had him wanting to change. Garret Henderson. He was envious of him in that Garret had shaken up his past, despite the invisible chains that must have tried to keep him bound.

That thought on its own gave him a slight pause. As hard as it was to admit, he had been acting like the injured party and seeing Garrett as the enemy in all this. This process had been doomed from the start.

So what if he ended up getting roaring drunk, getting into a fight and the next day found Ella, a woman he didn't give a snit about except care for like a little sister, in his bed! While another woman was missing!

Everything that he had gone through was a choice he made whether for good or to his detriment, hence it was time to look at this objectively, minus the perfect pastor he wanted to emulate, minus his mother who still cried when praying to God for him, to see the truth. His granny who still pinched his ears so he came back to his senses and stop being vengeful, and not to forget his dear old dad who hadn't been there in his life except in order to criticize him over his life choices. It was time he really thought over what he, Bill wanted out of life. It was time, he cleaned up his act.

"Oh my Bill you look so handsome," his mom said, his mind drifting to the present as she walked up to him with that smile he seemed to have gotten from her, full of humor and which appeared to make her look younger than her actual age.

"Uh mom, are you not meant to be checking up on the females." She swatted his arm when she got to where he stood and hugged him, before she appreciatively looked him over.

"Don't be silly...and miss out seeing my handsome son in his suit. Mm...mm..mm captain Lewis, you are about to make me a mother in law."

"You do have another handsome son remember," Denzel his older brother cut in. He hugged their mom and whispered. "Stop coddling him."

Bill winked at his brother. Of course he had heard that whisper which was deliberately loud for his ears. Denzel always claimed he turned that way because of their mother. Before their mother could linger with Bill, Denzel dragged her away while Bill sniggered at that little show of possessiveness. From then onwards it was like someone had removed the gentleman's fitting room sign on the door, because the women started getting into the room to view the dressed up mannequins, the groom, his brothers and his friends.

This wedding had better be over and done with, he had just had enough. Everyone was acting like it was the first wedding in the family. He could guess it was going to be with pomp and fun fair like the rest of the Fletcher weddings. Scandal free as to be expected. That *free* being in quotes and tinged with suspicion. In this case Cliff was getting married to a bloody heiress.

There were a few rumors going around on why he was doing it. Not that any of them held any truth in them since Cliff was a successful man in his own right. He had a financial firm that was making much more profit than they would have thought of Cliff as being capable of doing. Scratch that, let's face it.

They had seen that ingenious nature in him from when he was a child. How everything seemed to bloom beneath his fingers and the money increased in his hands while their pockets were always empty. In a nutshell, Cliff was a ruthless loan shark, who covered it up in tailor made suits and a sweet smile. So one of the rumors of him marrying Heather for her money was preposterous.

"My big brother looks good for the sampling," Marg said when she entered the room. She rushed to hug him, while Cliff huffed at that action and reached out to pull at her ears.

"Ouch," she yelped.

These two were something else. They still fought like eight year olds. Were they not aware that they were in their thirties now? He was laughing at their antics, fully aware that Marg had approached him so she pissed off Cliff by pretending like the groom wasn't important. He reached for the bottom button of his suit. Time to remove it. He was done for the day, pretending to be a mannequin to be looked at. He froze when his eyes caught sight of a pair of perfectly pedicured feet clad in strappy black heels next to Marg.

A slow tempo began in his heart, increasing the more as he lazily ran his eyes, frowning at the same time at what felt like endless, silky long legs before he came to the tiny red shorts that could only be worn by a daring woman. *Baby*, a voice whispered softly in his mind, that bs he had been spewing to his brothers of women not being his type, fleeing through the window like it hadn't been there. She was here.

The strappy top showed off the flat tummy. He skimmed her chest, the strap across barely covering her boobs, then the length of her neck and he came to the beautiful face with a nose ring on it. All in all, a beautiful, seductive package meant to send a man to hell. She had succeeded too. He went there and came back. It was still debatable though, his coming back that is.

"Hi," she greeted in her sultry voice and stared at him with that look that told him, she knew where his thoughts were, in the gutter and she would gladly join him. That became more apparent since she ran her eyes on him in the same manner he had on her and Bill sniggered. Bold, brazen-faced woman is what she was.

"Oh sorry, this is Innu, Innu—Bill," Marg hollered before she continued to talk with Cliff in muted tones.

Bill laughed. Thank God for little sisters like Marg, who managed to dampen the sizzle of physical attraction and make people aware of where they were.

"She is a handful," he commented.

Innu tilted her head slightly, still running her eyes over his face before a slow smile appeared on hers. "So you are the infamous brother." She took a slight step towards him. A glimmer of mischief in her eyes told him that this lady coming close must have been a handful as a child and unfortunately to every male in the vicinity she still was.

Bill grinned, and drew closer, "I gather you are the infamous friend who ran off with a designer to Italy on the day of her exams."

"Touché," she flapped her arms. "It was nice while it lasted."

Bill laughed. "How long have you been back in the city, heard from Marg that you were globetrotting and found yourself in France at one point, Antarctica—," his brow furrowed. "What in the hell would you be looking for there, I wonder—."

"That's easy, penguins," she cheerfully added.

"And not to forget Dubai." He finished with flourish. They were now standing close, her familiar sweet floral scent tickling his nostrils.

Innu lazily feigned out a yawn and replied. "Let's just say, I got tired of the international scene and came back home to roost, give and take, it's been a year."

"Hmm. Married."

"You wish," she rolled her eyes. "I find I prefer freaky than anything else." She had reached out to Bill to assist him in removing his tie. Apparently Marg, who knew that her brother and friend could at times be outrageous, had her ears trained on them even while chatting with Cliff. She whirled around to face the outrageous couple and swore, "Hell no," at their familiarity before she grabbed for her friend's hand and pulled her over.

"This is not good. Bill don't give her the time of day, she is Delilah's doppelganger. Just pretend you didn't hear what she said and when you see her in a few minutes from now, it will be like you've never met. As for you, Innu, pretend you didn't see what an incorrigible flirt Bill is. I can't believe you guys. Give him back the tie."

"But—," Innu protested and Marg furiously yanked the tie from her hand, handed it to him before she huffed at both of them then dragged Innu out of there.

Cliff looked at him and they both burst out laughing.

"I guess Marg is second guessing herself now since she was thinking you would help Innu with her little issue. That was mighty fast even for you."

Bill was laughing hard at that little episode, yet a disquietness had set in too. One he wasn't willing to pursue at the moment with everything that was going around.

What Cliff had just said made him pause from laughing. "Hey what?" He asked.

"What issue?"

Cliff sympathetically shook his head and walked away. Bill was about to follow him when a whack on the back had him stumbling. "I hope I didn't just see that. It's probably a dream. I probably must have dreamed up the train wreck that just happened."

Bill sniggered and folded his arms over his broad chest. "So—,"he drawled. "This is the delectable Innu."

Garret frowned at him. "No, this is troubled Innu up to mischief again."

"That woman seemed harmless," he lightly said. "I mean she didn't drag me out of here like you said she was capable of if she came across a handsome guy."

Garret groaned and his frown deepened. Bill nearly burst out laughing. It was rare to see Garret agitated over a person. Innu must have discovered the worrisome spot to press on Garret, just like his daughters and his wife did.

"Like I didn't witness how harmless you could be. I mean first meeting, you are already about to take the woman into your arms. Who does that?"

Again Bill quelled whatever he wanted to say and uttered instead. "Why do you need to act like it's not what you wanted to do when you first met Marg? I know—I know—you didn't act on it."

Bill was quite enjoying the horror that was now on Garrets' first. Things never ceased to amaze him, considering for once Garret appeared to have his tongue tied since he didn't have a rejoinder for the barb.

"Now Bill," Garret finally said, and raised his finger. Beulah got into the room at that same moment and announced to everyone to get changed before they met up at the Imperial hotel for their dinner and then she walked out of the room.

Bill patted Garret on the shoulder. "Save that thought for later, old man. Let me get changed and meet the future Mrs Lewis." He could hear Garret growl behind him. He laughed. This wedding was going to be much more fun than he had anticipated after all.

CHAPTER 4

"No missy, you sit here," Marg said to Innu once they got into the hotel restaurant and pulled her next to her.

"In no way are you sitting next to my brother. Both of you will give any person a heart attack."

Innu huffed. "This is silly Marg. That was like a mindless flirtation going on in there. Nothing more. Despite what you might think, I've changed."

"Have you met Jesus?"

"Not that change."

"Then you haven't."

Innu groaned. She reached out to a glass of water and gulped it down. Marg had been berating her ever since they walked out of that changing room like she had committed the worst crime in flirting with her brother.

Margaret's brother had totally taken her by surprise. The infamous Fletcher as he was called. Disowned by his father because of his lifestyle, nevertheless he still made something of himself, despite the lack of support from his family. He had totally taken her by surprise and left her floored. Her hands trembled but not from the revulsion or the fear she sometimes felt. Instead, her palms tingled and the sensation continued as she itched to have run her hands on him.

Her gaydor too wasn't flashing in Bill's case; in fact her naughty nature had come to the forefront, the one she had missed for quite some time now. The leisurely perusal he had given her from toe to head, his appreciation at what he was seeing even though she had been fighting a few misgivings over putting on that outfit. She had felt like a fraud. If she suddenly started wearing coveralls, Marg would surely start to ask over what was going on with her, so she had worn her former clothes, feeling like a tramp in them. In Bill's eyes she hadn't felt like a tramp at all.

Instead she had known she was a goner when his blatant perusal of her person didn't make her reach out for a printed wrap or leave her feeling naked and dirty as it usually did with others. For those moments when their eyes finally locked, she had felt empowered, an invisible thread binding them and she couldn't help it but draw close to him.

While others would have stayed far away from him, because for some reason he had this standoffish stance about him and of course Heather's bridesmaids had been talking about him too, planning on how to approach him, Innu had merely glided to him, following Marg and surprised at her sudden boldness.

How in the hell did Marg manage to hide him. Formidable looking and the tallest from among the Fletchers and to think she had thought it couldn't be possible.

Her first thought had been pro basketball player, then she saw the muscles, the suit failed to hide. He made her, a normal tall woman, feel like Marge the midget with Garret.

Her blood could still be felt thrumming and moving down her veins after that look and flirtation. Stunned over why she ran away from ordinary looking men and yet was drawn to him. Had she suddenly become one of those women who would thrill at the challenge of getting close to those men who had the lone air about them, despite the many people surrounding them?

In the few minutes she had gotten in the changing room Margaret's step mothers and some of the bridesmaids, as they went to take a look at the groomsmen, a time to mingle like Marg had described it as, Bill hadn't seemed like he noticed any of the young ladies but had merely spoken to his mother before he reached out for the buttons on his suit. Uninterested is what he had been.

"Even though I haven't met Jesus, that doesn't mean I haven't changed. There are a lot of things you don't know about me."

"Really." Marg folded her arms over her chest. "Like what."

"I no longer do one night stands. In fact I haven't been with a man for the past three years."

Marg stared at her in horror. Her mouth literally dropped open before she snapped it shut. She giggled. "Stop pulling my leg. You could have fooled me if it weren't for that angry guy at the airport. He had your lipstick on his lips by the way."

"Giles pounced and pawed at me Marg and I didn't ask for his attention."

"Ya right." She shook her head good humouredly like she hadn't heard her.

"Then why do you think I am out here searching for a husband."

"Boredom."

"What! Wait a minute. You said you would help me out and now you say I am doing this out of boredom. How could you help me out with that mindset?"

"Simple." Marg clasped her hand and answered. "I hoped that once you got to enjoy being married, you might stick it out in the long run. Funny too, for some reason I thought Bill might be the best in all this, considering the changes he recently made over his life. But after witnessing you two together. Nah ahh, hell no...it's a bad idea."

"Why may I ask?"

"You and Bill are both outrageous flirts. Your compatibility ends there. When you sleep with a guy Innu, you get bored easily, that's why a one night stand comes so easily to you. It's just meaningless, mind-blowing sex and you are done. Bill on the other hand commits. So I would hate to be torn between the two of you guys. Look at that man over there—," she pointed out to a handsome man who had just walked into the restaurant. "His name is Dylan."

"Too short," Innu said, cutting her off from going into a monologue over his good traits.

Marg waved her arms in defeat. "Ya, you're right. You've changed. Considering you have refused every man that I have presented to you so far. Yesterday's little get together was a flop." Marg narrowed her eyes on her and Innu rolled her eyes in return.

Yesterday she was too tired while Marg had insisted they hit the clubs, Innu's frequent places whenever she was in Harmony. That same feeling she had around Giles, she had felt it too in her so called frequent joints, and she had found herself avoiding guys she knew like a plague, while the nice, church guys that Marg knew made her feel more self conscious.

She'd slumped back on the chair but when she saw Bill get into the restaurant, laughing at whatever Garret was telling him, she sat up straight.

"Missy my brother is now off limits," Marg hissed.

Innu scoffed and ogled him up. A man comfortable in his own skin is what he was. Now dressed in another fancy Ethan Ross suit, tall, broad shouldered with that quirky smile that made him look younger than his years. The way the suit snuggly fit on him, she could already see it in her mind on how he would have any woman drooling when he put on his uniform. She bet he was one of those pilots who could lead a plane full of women to its doom and none of them would be any wiser. Bliss-full death is what they would experience, especially if he was to talk them through it.

"Innu!" Marg hit the table. Innu rolled her eyes and nonchalantly turned to face her.

"What. Am I not allowed to look even if he is now off limits? Tall guys are my Achilles heel mind you."

Marg huffed. Innu looked at Bill who also cast a cursory glance at her and winked. Garret and Marg both blanched before Garret did something that had Innu snorting in derision. He guided Bill far away from them as he possibly could, forgoing sitting next to his wife.

Really! Innu felt like protesting.

Cathy and her husband Ralph walked into the restaurant. Marg waved to them. Cathy reached out to Innu after she gave Marg a hug. The hug she offered Innu went on for much longer like they hadn't seen each for a long time while in actual fact they were together the previous night, in the clubs. Yep, a six month pregnant woman in a bar. Maybe that is why her night-out was a flop. With two married-pregnant women, what did one expect?

Cathy plopped down on the chair and took a gulp from Innu's water glass.

"Geez thanks a lot Cathy, what if it was wine, wouldn't that hurt the baby and then you would blame me for getting you into a miscarriage."

Cathy giggled at the exaggeration and patted her six month pregnancy. "Don't you pay attention to your senile aunt," she whispered to her tummy. "By the way, if that had been wine, I would have simply spit it in your face."

"Ha, ha." Innu rolled her eyes. She had known Cathy would say something like that. Once upon a time a sweet girl, hanging around Marg apparently was rubbing her the wrong way. She rubbed onto Marg and Marg rubbed onto the rest.

"What do you think?" Cathy pointed to a lean man, who was walking towards the other groomsmen.

Innu studied him. Right height like she usually preferred them and nothing. Not even a flicker. She stared at Bill who was listening to the chatterbox on his side. Apparently Garret had squeezed him between two bridesmaids, while he sat opposite him. Her heart fluttered. In excitement and irritation too, considering the two particular ladies are the same ones who had been debating over approaching Bill and laughing themselves silly that they intended to get laid while at the wedding.

Geez, doesn't anyone have morals, nowadays?

"Too lean, probably stringy down there and am not interested."

Cathy choked and Marg hissed, "Innu!"

"Oh my gosh, that water surely went down the wrong pipe," Cathy cleared her throat, her voice croaky after the coughing feat.

"Why are you not interested? It's unlike you to pass up a handsome face."

"She met Bill." Marg answered for her.

"Oh, the handsome captain Lewis. How did their first meeting go?"

"Disastrous. I don't think they will work."

"Really!"

"Guys I'm here." Innu pointed out to her two friends who were now talking over her. Why did people always do that? It was rude, except they appeared not to hear her because Marg continued to tell Cathy the whole unabridged version of her wanton behavior.

"Ooh my," Cathy was shaking her head now. "Still a hussy indeed."

"Now Cathy—." Innu looked at her best friends and waved them off. These two goody prudes were going to be the death of her. Especially when they would conveniently forget that they were terrible like her despite their so-called faith.

Marg tried to get Garret into bed when they were still dating and asked him to make love to her to prove that he was a man on their engagement day. She did everything else under the sun with him except for one thing, losing her virginity until they properly wedded.

Cathy on the other hand got pregnant before she even tied the knot. Innu counted the days for goodness sake after Cathy had her first child, Brandon, who was said to be a premature birth. Well that baby definitely didn't look seven months old when Innu saw him. Instead, he was fully developed and looked like he would get out of that crib and yell, *hey sweet cakes what's up mummy,* in a deep voice.

How she so missed Gina and wished for her to have been here, except Gina had gotten herself into a bloody motorbike accident and had a plaster on. The daredevil hadn't changed her ways in the least apart from having a rock on her finger. She still partied like crazy, courtesy of an understanding husband.

Funny story, Gina at twenty five decided she was off the game, no flings, no one night stands and threw away her skimpy wardrobe by replacing it with conservative clothes. She started going to church and within a year, she had met a medical doctor and gotten hitched. How did she do it?

According to her, when she was in church, she joined every association she could possibly join, participated in activities offered and of course wept her eyes out pretending to be filled with the Spirit. One gullible man took note of her and oooh, she held back the cookie until they wedded. Garret laughed over the story while she was screaming that she had succeeded before their bet was up.

Garret merely said to Gina, *you took God's principles, including going to church to find a husband. Why not look for a husband from those people you used to hang out with hmm. Because you knew you were so much alike and the behavior you exhibited wouldn't be good in building a happy home. So you said goodbye to the world's way, your worldly wise thinking and used God's principles instead. You changed the way you saw yourself, withheld the cookie for the right mate for you and despite all that pretending you had going on, fell hard for the guy after you truly gave your life to the Lord.*

Well boo hoo to Garret since he turned out to be right. Gina had indeed given her life to the Lord even though it all started as a game and a quest to get married.

Innu looked around the table, which was getting occupied at a slower rate than she would have liked and caught Bill staring at her.

A slight frown marred the intense look. She blushed. That couldn't be avoided even if she wanted to. When Marg had spelt out that he was now off limits to her, Bill on the other hand must have not received the memo on her being off limits to him, because right at that moment he was staring and not caring if anyone noticed that he only had his eyes on her. The gaze said it all. *We need more time to talk.*

She furiously fanned her face. Her body was heating up like someone had cranked a slow burning fire in her. "Do excuse me for a bit, I need the ladies," she whispered to Marg and nodded to Cathy before she left the table.

After Innu was done relieving her bladder and washing her hands, on her way back to the restaurant, her phone rang. She took it out from the back pocket of her shorts and smiled when she saw the caller ID.

"Nita darling, how are you?"

Nita was Margaret's niece and making strides in the modeling industry. Innu had requested the same favor from her like she had paused onto her aunt, in case Margaret's matchmaking fell short.

"Hi aunt Innu," Nita greeted her with a giggle, her voice low and sultry as usual. She had surely been taught by the best, Innu proudly thought. Considering, she's the one who tutored Margaret's niece on how to speak with a man and have his full attention. Very low to the point he would be forced to lean in and strain to hear her.

"Any good news for me." She slipped out onto the side door so she heard Nita better without Marg's interruption, which was likely to follow if she were to get back into the restaurant. She paused slightly with her leg in the air when she noticed which other person stood by the rail, slowly puffing out his smoke.

Bill.

She nearly swore and made the fast trot back inside. It was one thing to talk about other guys with his niece in the hotel and another to do so in his face. Wait a minute. Why did she have to be on the defensive? She and Bill had just shared a few words and extremely long side glances. *Do not forget we are back and rocking,* her hormones sang. She sighed, feeling the urge to slump back her shoulders in defeat.

Why him. She knew she had said a miracle, but this couldn't be it. Margaret's infamous brother!

Flirting was one thing.

But this man didn't seem like one she would wrap around her finger, even if she tried.

She stiffened her back. No use getting carried away.

Stepping out of the corridor, into the long lengthy balcony which had a few sun loungers scattered on it, she pretended not to see the man standing at the far corner and continued with her conversation with Nita.

"I'm sorry aunt Innu, but right now there is no one who's worthy to be by your side, the ones I managed to find...Aaah–they live a lot to be desired," Nita was saying.

"Really! I thought pretty faces would get the heat off me."

Nita giggled. "I don't think you would be attracted to the pretty faces out here. There are more girlish than boys." A flurry of beeps followed that had Innu taking the phone from her ear and looking at the screen.

"Hell no," she swore. The men more or less looked like boys that the general would eat for his lunch. Her eyes widened over one photo in particular. The beautiful smile, nicely coiled up black locks reminding her of Ethan Ross, minus the abs the man had, made her think, this is a girl. There was no way in which a guy would look that pretty, except for Ethan Ross of course whose features now bordered on rakish handsome with the scar on his brow. She flipped through more of the pictures, shaking her head in exasperation.

"I thought I would see more of the gung ho, macho type. What happened to those kinds of models?" She commented after she had gone through the gazillion photos Nita had just bombarded her with.

"Darling. Those kind are too busy working the fields to be on a modeling ramp. Today's look is more on how slender, adorable and popstarish one looks."

Innu snorted on that note. "Ok honey, thanks for trying."

"Byeee," Nita gladly screeched, dropping the seductive airs and making those smacking kissing sounds. Innu shook her head in mirth. Margaret's niece was something else, and from the deep voice she had heard addressing her before Nita hung up, that must have been her husband checking up on whether she was on her best behavior. She could bet Jay will be reprimanding his wife at this moment. Sliding back the phone into her pocket, she sighed.

An image of the general gloating over her failure filtered into her mind.

She rubbed her palms on the sides of her shorts and whirled around to face the man of the hour in her world.

Bill had already sensed her before she got onto the balcony. How could he not, when his senses had fired up from the moment he set his sight on her. He continued smoking nonetheless, pretending like she wasn't there, running his eyes broodingly at the view of Harmony below before his eyes ran to the mountains further away. He could hear her confidently walking towards him, her strides sure and steady before she reached him, plucked out the cig from his hand and smoked it.

He merely looked at her, as she drew the smoke into her mouth and produced lovely circles of smoke with her mouth, then received the cig back when she stretched her fingers to him. The slight brush of their fingers as he took the cig from hers, had her inhaling sharply, which he noticed but didn't point out to, wondering on what she was up to, having played dumb around all the people in the changing room.

Where were you all this time?

"I didn't think I would find you out here. Don't tell me you are tired of those bridesmaids that you were squeezed between by Pastor Gee."

I was waiting for you.

"That's actually the reason why I'm out here. I can't bear being the center of attention. But I'm sure in two minutes' time; Henderson will be popping his head out here to check on my whereabouts, so he fosters my presence on other unsuspecting women."

"Funny," she giggled. Bill handed her the cig and she drew in a breath, and then looked at it.

"I sure could do with something stronger than this though."

Bill slowly shut his eyes and opened them, then pasted one of his easy smiles even though he felt like his jaw would break at any moment, from the grinding of the teeth that he was trying to avoid. "I don't have weed on me, if that's what you are implying."

"Euuew, I didn't ask for that. Weed damages the brain cells, I don't smoke that stuff." Her beautiful contrite expression had him asking, "Really," as he stubbed out the cig and faced her. His eyes studied her for a slight moment, looking for a hint of recognition to surface, but nothing. She merely fidgeted with her hair. He should have known. Marg and Garret were right. Innu did forget the men she had ever been involved with including him. The fact that he was her best friend's brother didn't seem to make a difference.

He had been taken by surprise when he saw the beautiful feet. He wouldn't have missed them in any way, including the little toes that appeared to have little nails, which she had griped about.

"Yah, really." She said defensively.

"So if I'm to give you this—you will not accept." Her eyes widened when he removed a joint out from his pocket. He winked at her, guessing that she had totally been taken by surprise.

"It's not the strong stuff you need, but it will give you a little boost," he finished with a shrug.

"Marg was right. You're terrible. Let me rephrase that part. We-are-both-terrible."

Tell me about it.

Bill laughed and lit the joint then he handed it to her. Innu smoked deeply and exhaled through the nose. "Do you want to?"

Bill shook his head. "I still need my brain cells intact."

She choked on the smoke and coughed. "I can't believe you said that and with a straight face. Is that how you get people hooked on this stuff?"

Bewilderment tinged her voice while Bill shook his head and answered, "I no longer do that. Once upon a time– maybe. But I just thought you needed this. That conversation you were having sounded intense."

He was fishing for clues but nothing so far, like she was a different person altogether. The flash, Garret had once said about her, exchanging men like her dresses and with no compaction over right and wrong. To her it was okay, as long as she got the attention she needed for that moment.

Then why did he feel like right now he would want to be that dress again. As it was, he was holding tightly onto his control, damning the Fletcher genes that longed to get her naked and in bed in no time at all.

"Ha ha, says the man who was acting all nonchalant about it—I gather Marg told you about my search for a husband."

Bill froze for a moment. *What. Huh.* His libido suffered a slow death there.

"Husband—search." He slowly said and looked at her in the eyes then nodded.

"Geez, I wonder if I should bury myself six feet under or what. This was meant to be a secret. But from what I'm seeing here, she might have told everyone."

There was a slight pause of silence as Innu came to grips with the fact that her best friend was something else. In her mind, she was already yanking out her hair from her scalp. For a shrink, Margaret Henderson was turning out to not be aware of the meaning of discrete.

The reason why Innu hadn't broadcasted her wish to settle down in the first place, was because of her little issues and the fact that she had decided that none of this was going to be real.

She and the so-called husband would have to convince the general that they were a happy couple, get hitched and live separate lives in private. One year would be enough for her to sort out her business and by that time she would not need the extra money and the man would be out of the door. A temporary husband would do just fine in her case.

"I have a confession to make." Bill plucked out the joint from her hand and took a smoke. Innu smiled since a while ago he had said he didn't want to fry his brain cells, guess the confession needed fortification. She waited, watching him beneath her long lashes and received the joint he handed to her after a long pull that had him coughing.

"I wonder how you're able to take this stuff."

She giggled. "You're a smoker Bill, remember." He laughed then he wagged his finger in her face. "I mean you're the first woman I've met who appears to be able to handle this, and sound sober still. Ok, confession time, are you ready?"

Innu couldn't help but chuckle in glee. So far their conversation seemed to be light enough, even though she had eaten him up in her mind a thousand times. Compounded with this little stunt, she was certainly about to eat him up in reality. She stopped smoking a few years ago due to health reasons and all because of this man, she had started again.

"Here goes."

You want to help me and be my husband.

"Marg didn't say a thing."

Her mouth sagged open in shock. Then clamped shut at the knowing look that he gave her.

"Oh...ooooh."

Of course, she had been dumb enough to say that just a while ago.

"Aah, I'm frazzled. That's why 'the' little blurting. Do you mind?" She waved between them. For some reason she felt comfortable in his presence, like she would speak her mind without him judging her.

"Mind what. I think marriage is a noble thing to do."

She slowly stubbed out the joint and decided what the heck, since he wasn't offering like the gentleman she had thought him to be, then she should.

What were they doing? Were they twelve, to be standing by the rails, chatting like they weren't this chemistry going on and she had literally placed an offer that would make them go into another level with their flirtation.

You go girl, her insides said in quivers, rejoicing that the traumatic experience at least hadn't left her hopelessly numbed after all. They were guys out there who still could turn her innards to mash.

She raised her eyes and squarely looked at him. "Marriage is noble if entered into for the right reasons. Mine aren't that."

A frown marred his features and she found herself resisting hard the urge to press the frown down with her fingers till it vanished. She turned away and rubbed her neck instead, feeling the tension on it. She knew he shifted closer to her because her breath hitched up a notch further and heat enveloped her as the sizzle of attraction that had been there intensified.

"May I." His breath fluttered near her neck and she sighed in relief. A slight nod, then she gasped as he chuckled. "Don't worry love. I won't drop you. I just want you to stand at a slightly higher place."

The endearment easily slid from his mouth. She giggled, trying to dispel the nervous energy and waited. Already giddy from that little effortless picking episode. It felt like an eternity even though it was just a few brief seconds. Her tummy knotted up in anticipation and her back stiffened while she fought dismally against the temptation to lean back on him for support.

What was happening to her? She wondered again. Even in her best of days, she had never been sexually wound up this much. Yes, she was one of those girls who had been taught from early on that sex was bad for them, but nevertheless did the opposite.

That one touch on her neck released the breath she hadn't been aware she was holding. A flurry of butterflies rose in her tummy and she hoped to God she hadn't moaned when she felt his warm hands and deft fingers work on her neck then shoulders, the touch so familiar as she gave in to the urge and sagged back into his arms.

The Fletcher touch. She just knew it. Marg had spoken about it, in that it made anyone putty in the hands of a Fletcher if one of them ever used that on their partner. From all standpoints, this was a simple massage. Maybe it was just her who had gone on a drought for so long that she was now latching onto the first man who appeared to strip her of those misgiving and fears that had bound her for the past years, she reasoned. Even though that couldn't explain the familiarity. She released another moan, arching her back as Bill's expert fingers trailed on her back. They pressed, kneaded, caressed, and taunted, all at the same time.

"This feels so damn good," she whimpered. Bill chuckled in response before she reluctantly released another moan. A total wreck is what she was.

"Tell me about your not so noble reason to want to get married," he commanded softly, his breath fluttering on her neck, exposing the thickened layer she once thought she had developed, to be nothing but sensitive skin waiting to combust and go aflame under expert fingers. She knew at that moment they stood too close than was appropriate for two strangers. If Marg and Garret were to get onto the balcony while Bill massaged her, she knew they would both scream the roof down, including making them take a fast trip to the altar.

Bill's scent and warmth reached out to her in an embrace, curling around her in a cocoon before he wound one arm around her waist so she wouldn't topple over and fall, her rubbery legs giving in to the sensations she was now feeling.

Oh my word—this wasn't a simple massage. She'd thought she was mistaken. No. Bill was definitely doing something to her which made her want to stretch and let him continue with kneading some parts too that had long been out of use.

His fingers pried her flesh, her tense muscles releasing at his touch like they were nothing. He knew how to touch her and receive the result he wanted, a ball of quivering mass ready to utter the damned words, *take me to bed.*

You should know better, it never ends well, her mind mocked and she disregarded its warning. She turned around to face Bill instead, the reasons for wanting to get hitched, having flown out of her mind, just like that.

No coherent thought was filtering in. Her breath was coming out in little faint gasps, from the little seduction with the hands that had just taken place and that was still taking place, seeing Bill continued massaging her shoulders, intent on the task at hand like he was oblivious to how her boobs now pressed against his chest, and oblivious to how their thighs pressed against each other, his hard and hers soft.

If it wasn't for the tell-tell sign she had felt pressing on her back and which had made her turn around and face him, the expression he was wearing would have told her that Bill felt nothing. She was the crazy one, aroused beyond measure. She slid her hand down his face and he froze, stared deeply into her eyes, with a question then gruffly said, *"Baby."*

Hell, he could call her whatever he deemed fit. Baby, love, sweetheart, honey, she would gladly receive all those titles as long as he finished what he had started. Seeing him looking at her intensely and not taking the final move, Innu did that for him. She leaned in and kissed him, ran her tongue on the seam of those full lips, before she slid her tongue in like she had a right to do so.

Bill stood still, unresponsive on all accounts. He was most probably taken by surprise at that bold move, or he was contemplating on what to do with the woman who had thrown herself into his arms, when he was offering her a simple massage which to her had seared through, thawed and melted whatever ice she had going on.

She was literally quivering with need and it was *all his fault*. Her wanton body had already run ahead and was now plastered on him as it possibly could be, her slender hands cupping his head and longing for the deepening kiss that was bound to make her go up in flames.

The inaction on Bill's part made her pull away, considering he wasn't encouraging her to continue at the seduction he had started with the glorious massage. Bells rang all around over her little blunder. Apart from being stuck in an isolation chamber where emotions were concerned for these years, it appeared her senses had all dulled down too where desire was concerned, because this man she was draped against had an iron will and wasn't one to give into the urges his body detected. A touch from his strong arms on her back when he sensed her pulling away had her reeling as he took charge of the kiss.

She released a moan of delight from that simple action. The kiss was certainly not like her clumsy attempt she had pulled out a while ago. In the same way the fingers had expertly un-knotted her muscles, there wasn't any of the awkwardness that Innu could have anticipated at first kiss, only a natural melding as their tongues mated, tasted and a delicious sweetness swept through her body. Bill nibbled lightly on her lips, eliciting a few giggles. His lips took possession of hers once again as they ignited a flame throughout her body that she'd never experienced with any other man.

For a brief moment she forgot where she was and what remained was the strength of his hold, the heat of his body and that incredible mouth that moved on hers with such possessiveness, sure in every way that he had her where he wanted her to be. This felt like heaven, she thought and wrapped her arms around his neck, letting the lovemaking to her lips have its full run as parts of her body ached for attention too. She wasn't disappointed at all since he gave her what she craved. Cradled her bottom close to him, making her feel his arousal on her tummy and nearly making her hyperventilate when he lovingly ran his hand on her behind.

Being close to him in this way, in his strong arms, made her feel like she rightfully belonged there and that this was the place she would want to always be for the rest of her life.

A flicker of another place and time passed through her mind, the scent of his subtle cologne mixed with sandalwood, tickled her nose, while the same lean fingers expertly thrummed her up like a spanish guitar, had her abruptly pulling away and looking at him in horror.

"I...I–,"her words stumbled. "I'm sorry. I didn't mean to do that."

Bill stood transfixed where Innu had left him after her frantic push. She clutched on her chest, still horrified like what she had done a while ago isn't something she would normally do.

He missed her so badly in his arms, like he missed her three years back when they first met, on that disastrous night which he failed to talk about till to date. From the way Innu was acting, it probably meant she hadn't mentioned anything to Marg, but rather was pretending that they were complete strangers, who could just fall into a familiar routine like it was nothing.

"Innu–baby," he said her name, shook his head slightly to clear his mind, and was ready to utter the words we *need to talk*. That is when he noticed her still clutching at her chest. She stared at him with a horrified look and contritely said, "I didn't mean to throw myself at you in that manner. I swear."

Bill would have laughed on that note, calling her bluff and to stop pretending. The time was up, except the look of horror, didn't seem like pretense, but more of someone on the verge of panic. Her eyes rolled over and her breath came in soft gasps as she tried to breathe in more air into what must have felt like constricted lungs.

Bill swore and moved fast to where she had scrambled to in her frantic escape from being near him and swept her off her feet. He walked fast to the nearest sun lounger on the balcony and engulfed her in a hug, saying soothing words near her ear and impersonally running his hand on her back. Offering comfort and not seducing her like before. She tried to flay her arms but he held them fast and steady, not letting go of them. Terror marked her beautiful features as she blankly looked at him like she was no longer here but somewhere else, where he might not be able to reach her until the wave passed.

"Please don't hurt me," she whimpered. "Hush love." He softly said. "I'm here; no one is going to hurt you." He continued speaking to her in that same gentle voice as her body shuddered.

Innu could feel the dark cold hands trying to claw her under as fear set it. She had to get out of there and fast. She whimpered softly. Faint voices could be heard, menacing by all means as they drew closer to her and she quaked in fear. From one who could have lost the fight and given in to the darkness that cloistered her up to the point she failed to breathe and her chest hurt so bad, a voice seemed to drift through the dark fog.

Gentle, soothing and a balm to her frayed nerves.

"Breathe sweetie," the deep voice commanded softly and she did just that. When she inhaled and exhaled deeply, warmth flooded through her body as the scent of sandalwood took over and she sagged in relief in his arms.

Bill continued to run his hand on her back in slow motions while Innu clutched hard on his neck and wept. Curled up in a ball in his arms like a child and not the mature woman she was. It took a while for her to quiet down.

Bill knew when Innu became aware of where she was and in whose arms. Just like he suspected, she scrambled off his lap and stood up in a daze like one about to flee.

He stood up too and grabbed her hand. "We need to talk."

She shook her head. "No."

"Yes." He slowly nodded. She fearfully looked at his arm and he let her go.

"I am not going to hurt you. I just need us to talk." He slid his hand into the pocket to retrieve a clean hanky then handed it to her. Innu warily looked at him.

"Take it." She took it and wiped her tears.

"Care to share what happened just right now."

Innu shook her head again and wiped her face before she straightened her spine. "There is nothing to talk about. I guess what just happened comes with age. Emotional woman on the loose, that kind of thing." Her voice was steady and if he had been someone else, he would have believed her and not caught the tremor at the end.

"Uh huh and nothing to do with failing to keep up with the game you are playing."

She frowned at him. "This...this is a bad idea. I should go." She dashed out of the balcony like someone was out to get her for revealing too much so far.

"Innu!" Bill bellowed and followed after her. Garret stopped him as he got into the corridor and he helplessly watched her rush into the ladies restroom. He would have followed after, to confront her except for the hand on his shoulder.

"Bill, where were you? Everyone is looking for you." One look from Garret and he removed his clean hanky from his pocket and handed it to him.

"Getting a breather. Am I not allowed to do that?"

"It must have been some breather indeed, considering you're smeared in lipstick."

Bill rolled his eyes and took the proffered hanky that he used to wipe his face.

"Better now," he asked. Garret nodded. "You will do."

Bill knew why Garret had come out to look for him, in the same manner Garret assumed on why he had vacated the room abruptly in the first place. *Fletcher.*

Except Fletcher wasn't in his mind at that particular moment, but his little sister's best friend.

Garret knew that he couldn't be in the same room with Fletcher and pretend that everything was okay, especially when he would give him those sneering looks. While the rest of his brothers didn't mind how their father disdainfully treated them. Bill has always been the vocal one in the lot. His outspokenness as a kid had put him in more trouble too than the other boys where Fletcher was concerned. How a man could be such an infuriating ass all the time and would get away with it, he had wondered.

"Has dinner ended, including the speeches?"

Garret was still watching him, with that raised brow, before his eyes would stare at the shut door to the ladies restroom.

"Really. Has it come to a point where you need to be in the same vicinity with your father for just a second?"

"Don't call that man my father."

Garret raised his arms in defeat. "Easy. Dinner and the speeches haven't yet started. Let's go back in there and we get this over and done with. Cliff needs you... I gather you and Innu were getting to know each other well."

A dark scowl set on his features that had Garret shaking his head before he opened his mouth to comment.

"Save it," Bill retorted. Garret scoffed. He knew where his thoughts were heading to at the moment and he didn't want to say anything that would land him into more landmines.

Once he had figured out what was happening, then would he be able to answer everything.

"You're right. Let's get this over and done with." He muttered and watched Garret narrow his eyes on him before he shrugged his shoulders and they walked back to the restaurant.

"WHAT'S GOING ON," MARG asked Innu after she sat back on the chair. It had taken her a while to get back into the restaurant after her little episode with Bill. She had sat in the restroom for quite a while after she freshened up on her makeup, contemplating to call it quits and head home.

She was utterly stunned and scared. Stunned that she had responded in that manner to Bill, scared over how he had gotten under her skin without trying and both stunned and scared over how quickly he had almost come to know the truth about her.

Right now the so-called brother to her best friend wasn't looking her way. Should she be relieved over that, she wondered. He smiled at something one of the ladies on his left side said. Even though further away from her, she could tell that the smile was on the surface and did not reach those remarkable black eyes.

"Nothing, just had to make a quick call to nana. What did I miss?" she asked, trying to scrub up the concern that something was wrong with Bill, he just seemed so wound up and tense. A preposterous thought indeed considering she had her own issues to deal with.

Marg smiled. "Nothing, apart from the usual family drama."

Innu smiled back then nodded to the waitress who promptly delivered the seven colored meal to her and left.

Marg was now enjoying the fruit salad and quickly began to regale her over the tasks that she needed to complete before the big wedding tomorrow.

Cathy was chatting with her husband, and from the few snatches Innu caught from their conversation, she was emotionally blackmailing Ralph. "The baby is tired and needs to go home," she whined.

Innu rolled her eyes and Marg laughed when she caught her doing so.

"By the way, that was a mighty long call to your nana. Did you know Bill was out for a long time too? When he came back into the restaurant, he almost removed me from my seat so I got one next to my husband. It was when I asked him why he smelt like you and the missed lipstick smudge on his shirt that he retreated."

Innu choked on her food. Marg smiled and handed her a glass of water.

"Drink." She motioned.

Innu huffed at the sweet smile, more like the barring of her teeth. She didn't look pleased at all.

"I hope you didn't get laid in the few minutes or was it in the hour you were absent from the table."

"Marg!"

Marg stared at her like she hadn't said anything offensive.

"Marg what?"

"I am not that fast." Innu mumbled beneath her breath.

"You could have fooled me."

Innu grabbed for her fork that had clattered on her plate. Her fingers trembled. Gosh, how was she going to go through this without revealing to everyone what a fool she was? She needed her medication and fast, except she hadn't carried them since she thought she would brave it somehow.

"Are you ok?" Marg narrowed her eyes at her trembling hand. Innu placed the other on top of it and took them both back, placing them on her lap.

"Chirpy.You know me darling. A klutz at times."

A quick glance on Bill showed that the girl on his right was leaning to his side like she had a secret to tell him and was whispering about it near his ear. For goodness sake, were these ladies not going to stop? The guy wasn't interested. He only was interested in her; she vehemently thought and fisted her hands on her lap, resisting the urge to get up from her chair and holler, oii, stop doing that.

Mr. Jonathan Price, the bride's father stood up from the chair and motioned by clicking on the wine glass with a fork that he wanted to say a few words.

The noisy room quieted down.

"Good evening to you all."

"Evening Mr. Price," was the resounding answer he got. He smiled. "Just a brief thank you to all of you for coming to join me and my family on this happy occasion and especially on such a short notice. I've known Cliff for a while now, the ruthlessness he can employ when he is doing business and I happen to be one of the few men who know that he is not all that, but he also has a gentle nature for the underdog, a deep respect for women and very very unwavering loyalty to those he deeply cares for. Despite the wedding being made in a rush, I wouldn't have made a better choice for my princess than him and I believe he will always put Heather's needs above everything else. To Cliff and Heather."

"To Cliff and Heather," everyone said in unison as they clicked their glasses in a toast.

"Are those chocolate coated words actually land mines or what? It felt more like a threat to me." Innu whispered to Marg who giggled and swatted her arm. She had felt Marg's probing gaze on her, hence had said that to disarm her.

"Drop it if you know what's good for you. There's nothing to speculate here, Heather and Cliff are in love." Marg pointedly looked at the couple and Innu followed her gaze. The couple seemed happy by all means, especially when Cliff reached out to Heather's hand on the table and squeezed it in assurance. Heather looked up to Cliff and smiled. The love was evident for all to see, before she mouthed. "I love you."

Wow. Apparently that still existed for some folks.

Their table was at the front, the families having reserved the use of the whole restaurant for dinner.

"Indeed Cliff is the model son," Fletcher said and he stood up from his chair. Innu giggled since Marg had mumbled beneath her breath, "oh, brother here we go."

"As you know Jonathan, being a parent is a daunting task and at times no matter how much you try, they will always be the black sheep in the family, who go against the fundamentals of nature."

Bill's mother Claudine was taking a sip of water. She choked and started coughing, while Dorothy and the rest of the wives warningly looked at Fletcher. Since Innu had been around most of the family members before, she knew what that threat signaled.

She stared at Bill who furiously glared at Fletcher like he would go up to him and wipe the floor with his face. She shivered at the murderous look. He released a snorting sound and his brothers gave him the same warning look the women were giving to their husband.

"And that is our cue to leave," Marg leaned in and whispered near her ear. "You will not like this and where it's going." Motioning to her Cathy, Cathy gladly stood up, being assisted by her husband and they walked out of the room.

"Innu," Marg growled, and tugged at her sleeves. She pointed to the door when Garret looked at her.

"I'm definitely not staying for this," Josephine was heard saying, then she stood up from her chair and walked up to the table at the front where the bride and groom sat. She whispered something to her son who nodded to Heather and they both left. Not that Fletcher noticed since his eyes were intent on skinning the black sheep of the family alive.

"Bill, what's that snort for? If you have nothing good to say, keep those snorting sounds to yourself." He changed his bellow to a sweet voice and continued, "You see, like I was saying, usually some children are just too black to even care about their families reputation. They make you wonder if they are even yours."

Innu gasped in shock. Did he just say that? As if Bill was outraged in the same manner as her, he abruptly stood up from the chair and flipped it away like it was nothing. His mom rushed to him.

"Fletcher, you have no right to say that to my mother's face," he bellowed.

"Bill, it's okay," his mother said, clutching on his arm.

"No mom, it's not okay. He can't belittle you like this because of me and to top it all, in front of these strangers."

The guests, who had been stunned for a moment by the eruption of violence and drama slowly unfolding in their midst, scrambled for cover, leaving behind those strong enough to handle Bill and Fletchers fight.

"Innu," Marg desperately pulled at her sleeve. "You will not like where this is going. Let's go," she hissed. Innu grabbed a drink instead, and could hear Marg huff on her side before she plopped back on the seat. It's not like she was trying to be difficult. What Marg hadn't realized was that she was trembling in her strappy heels like a bucket of ice cold water had been poured over her body.

She was looking at a furious Bill and got chillingly struck by her tumultuous emotions when she found that side of him sexy as hell. What she needed was a psychiatrist and fast.

Marg had mentioned that the two men couldn't handle each other, what she failed to say in the few words she spoke about her estranged brother was that Bill hated his father with passion. This most likely explained why Bill had been on the balcony instead of in the restaurant. For some insane reason she thought he had been waiting on the balcony for her. Now it was evident that he had been seeking a semblance of calm when he was staring at the mountains and taking a smoke. The tension in the restaurant appeared to make the huge room shrink in size since it was so thick that one needed a knife to cut through it.

Fletcher turned away from the glare he was getting from Bill and said to Price, "You see my son in law here, prayer is all it took and he is in love with his wife like he was never in any way attracted to men."

"Da!" Marg snapped and abruptly stood up from her chair.

"What, isn't it true, your husband doesn't mind my talking about it, why should you."

"There's a time for discussing some of these things and it's definitely not over dinner with strangers."

"Jonathan will be family by tomorrow. He has the right to know," he barked in answer at her, before he turned to Jonathan again, still grasping the damned wine glass in his hand. "You see, at other times you have more than two black sheep in the family."

Marg snorted in derision and walked out of the room. Garret slightly smiled to the guests who still remained before he followed after his wife.

"Now that's what I meant, very good indeed. He sees the wife in distress and follows to comfort her. Right...back to my speech."

The brothers could be heard growling, while Godfrey and Leo held fast onto Bill's shoulders.

"The fruit never lands far from the tree. Black sheep only reveal that the parent is black," Bill said. His father glared at him.

"What would you know when you will never have children of your own. Prancing around town like a woman. A disgrace is what you're."

"Yes, indeed what would I know Fletcher. At least I don't have the burden of passing on my failures to the so-called line. Who are you, to think you are any better. For your information, it takes more than being a sperm donor to be a father."

"Bill!" his father bellowed and the veins of his forehead could be clearly seen like they were about to burst forth.

Ook, Innu stood up then. This was getting darker with both men now facing each other and throwing those fiery darts directly. She should have left with Marg, instead of listening to all this stuff, except... She bit hard on her bottom lip, her mind yelling, RUN, while her heart told her to be there. So, for once in her life, she took heed to the voice in her heart instead and walked up to Bill and his brothers.

"By the way, I am better than you in every way. One thing I was able to do that you never were, is to commit to a person regardless of whether they were male or female."

His father sneered. "Female my foot, like you ever tried those before. Who in hell would want your attention after she realizes the kind of man that you're. Disgusting in every way."

Bill's brothers clutched him harder on his shoulders because he was now dragging them along with him to wipe that sneer from Fletcher's face. Two things happened simultaneously that took all of the family members by surprise. A touch on Bill's chest, where his heart beat so fast and a voice, clear as day, was heard over the noise as it said his name. Bill.

Godfrey and Leo let go of Bill when Innu barred his path, because from being furious, that single touch had done something both their hold on his shoulders had failed to, calmed him down. Innu stared into his eyes, pleading with him that he not take the last step of no return.

With her eyes still looking at him, his heart furiously thumping beneath her palm, she slid her hand from the chest, moved to his side and then slipped her fingers into Bill's.

Everyone gasped at the familiarity.

"Fletcher, I'll have Bill any other way. I don't care who he has been with, what he has been up to. That to me is all in the past. He is not disgusting at all–but has a beautiful soul and is the love of my life," she said, stunning Fletcher and everyone else.

One side of her brain that was still functional kept on saying, how could this man be so cruel to his son. Bill who had soothed and comforted her on the balcony wasn't disgusting like he put it. This old man was that.

"You!" Fletcher yelled, staring at her in disbelief. Innu flinched and Bill held her fast, slightly shielding her.

"Yes her," he confidently cut in. "I am marrying her and rest assured that we will have beautiful babies who will know that they are loved and never in any way will they be made to feel like freaks of nature."

"This is a joke right," Fletcher said. "You're both out of your minds."

"Just stop it!" Beulah yelled. She had banged the table, nearly toppling over Gordon's drink since he was seated next to her. He grabbed it and muttered, "I'm not losing good scotch over this."

"Can't we have just one normal meal without you biting your heads off each other? Look around you." Beulah motioned with her hands. "Are you the only guests in this restaurant?" She slid the chair away and stood up. "Hopefully you bring your best game to the church, for the rehearsal, if not, both of you stay the hell away from Cliff and Heather's wedding. This is supposed to be a happy occasion and we will damn ensure it will be that, minus your usual drama."

Like a queen, with the full attention of her subjects, Beulah finished, apologized to Jonathan and walked up to a dazed Innu who was still stunned by what she had just done and holding fast to Bill like her life depended on it.

"Welcome to the family dear. I always believed Bill would come around. He is a good man."

Fletcher snorted and her brows furrowed on him in a frown. "Despite—what anyone might tell you. I know you saw that in him, or you wouldn't have stepped in like this." She finished, wrapped Innu in a hug, pulled back and glided out of that restaurant.

Shit, what in the hell have I just done, Innu almost yelled. She nearly grabbed Margaret's mom's skirt and hid under them.

What in the hell had she done? She shivered slightly. Bill looked at her with concern.

"A toast to the new couple," a drunk Gordon said with a chuckle before he took a gulp of the scotch now safely in his hand.

Bill scoffed. "Junkies and drunkards are now considered good model citizens, you did a great job in raising them Mr. Fletcher." He dragged Innu out of there, while his father yelled a few obscenities over him being the worst mistake he ever made.

Once outside, Bill didn't stop and let go of her hand, but led her to the lift that was opening at that moment. They got in; he pressed the number to his floor and leaned on the wall then shut his eyes, his breathing harsh even to her ears. Innu tried to let his hand go but he tightened his hold, so she shrugged her shoulders and leaned back. What was the use of fighting when at the moment he probably wasn't seeing her, but was thinking about his huge fight with Fletcher, even though that flicker of concern in there had told her he was aware that she was scared.

They got to his floor and he led her to his room, slid the key card in its slot, opened the door then shut it behind them. The bang seemed to echo its finality. She was now alone with an angry man to calm down. Once the door was shut, instead of what she had thought, Bill simply let go of her hand and walked to the huge bed that dominated the room, sat on it and cradled his face in his hands.

Innu released a sigh and looked around. Definitely a bachelor pad is what it was. From what Marg had said, Bill didn't set roots. He did a lot of traveling even when it wasn't necessary and his life was spent living in hotels. She slowly walked deeper into the room, her knees still shaky from that whole drama that had played out, looking at the framed picture on the wall of Bill in different places, with colleagues, with friends and some with his mom, brother and step siblings.

There was one with his nieces. His love was shining through the pic for them. Lucy had wrapped her little arms on his neck while he held baby Gail in his arms. Gail must have been a day or a few hours old, she thought, since part of Margaret's hand could be seen and the hospital band was still on her wrist.

"That went well." Innu finally said with a chuckle, trying to disperse the awkward situation she now found herself in.

Bill snapped his head up, like he was suddenly aware of her presence for the first time since he got into his room.

"What happened?"

She smiled. "Well–we. No." She shook her head and walked up to where he sat. "You announced to everyone that we will be getting married and in future we will have beautiful children who will be loooved."

"Oh hell."

"It's bad to swear, especially around our future children." Bill narrowed his eyes on her. He threw back his head and laughed after he saw the look she wore.

"Better now," she asked and tentatively felt his forehead with the back of her hand. She was standing close, her eyes searching deeply into his. The pain she had seen in his eyes and that had propelled her to make an utter fool of herself was now masked from her view. Bill pulled her close as she whispered. "Fever down, I was afraid I was about to lose you to it. You know heads explode when you get too furious."

She cradled his head and continued to stand where he had pulled her to. His head on her flat tummy while her hand soothingly ran in his hair.

"You are never serious. I guess that's why you and Marg get along pretty well and have been friends for this long."

She pouted her lips. How could he say that, when she had just ventured into the adult territory with her little announcement, serious was her second nature from now on?

Bill pulled away then stood up from the bed. He held up her hand, sliding her fingers into his. Innu's breath hitched.

"Bill."

For a moment, Bill stared into her beautiful brown eyes at a loss. He still searched deeply into them, still confused over what was happening. The panic attack was a hint that something must have happened to her after their night together. No recognition still. Could she be this cold? Then his mind too drifted to the scene in the restaurant. Ok, he was way more confused than before on what was going on with her.

Let it be for now. She is here. He assured himself.

"Do you want to back away from all this?"

"What?" Innu stared at Bill in confusion. For a second there, she was a goner and all she longed for was for him to lean over and kiss her. For some reason she missed his kiss, having experienced it the first time just a mere two hours away. How could it be possible? Did he brand her or what? That was preposterous.

Marg had told her about the Fletcher touch, but there was nothing like that. It simply wasn't possible.

His body heat had encompassed her, seeping through every pore of her body and she stared at him in wonder. When she was meant to be running away, panicky on all accounts, here she was, looking deeply into his eyes, searching for the missing piece of the puzzle on why she seemed to want this man happy, why Fletcher's words had hit her hard than possible and for the love of God, why she felt so safe around him.

"I mean back down from what I said in the restaurant."

She shook her head and said with a chuckle. "I'm in search of a husband, remember.

Even though I had set myself up for a husband who will be willing to settle for a platonic relationship, this is so much better.

So this is cool."

He grinned and tugged at his tie. Innu reached out to help him remove it. She also reached out to remove the jacket, letting it slowly slide over his strong arms to the bed while she ran her hand on his hard broad chest. A grasp of her hand that was on the chest, made her freeze.

Bill intertwined his fingers with hers, leaned in and kissed her hand, before moving up the arm.

"Speaking about what I said. What was that? You said a lot too." She chuckled as she tugged her hand away. Wasn't he aware of what he was doing to her with those little kisses over her arm?

Heat had set in every pore, which would change into a fiery inferno if she let it take her to where there seemed to be heading to and at a very fast rate.

Innu wrapped her arms on his neck instead and was delighted when he finally leaned down to give her the kiss she was longing for. He took his time like before, possessing her lips, nipping at them playfully then he deepened the kiss. *Oh my,* a slight moan was released from deep down her throat as he ran his hand on her back. If she had thought the first time was a fluke, then she was wrong, her whole being wanted him. Bill groaned and pulled back.

"A breather. This is moving way too fast for my liking."

Oh no, this is moving quite slow actually.

She giggled and cupped his face before she gave him one last lingering kiss and pulled away.

"You are right. Time up."

"Umh." Bill slightly shifted and placed his hands into the pockets. Guess she too had the same effect he had on her.

"What kind of husband is it that you are looking for? You did say you were on a husband search before you ruined everything by announcing to everyone that you were in love with me. I mean that is a mighty leap even for you. From total strangers to instant—lovers. Does that normally happen in your life?"

Where a while ago she was content in pulling away and still remaining close to him, not touching but his very being embracing her, when he asked that, she did shift, retreating to the study table that was at the corner of the room.

Her instincts seemed to now be fired up too, because it was like she anticipated his response, even before she uttered the words that she was about to.

She feigned indifference, which she wasn't feeling, sat on the chair and crossed her legs.

She ignored everything else he had said apart from one. "Umh. A temporary husband will do."

"Temporary." A deathly silence fell in the room. It was unnerving, considering her whole being seemed to have been aware of what would happen.

She found herself stuttering in her answer and looking at him like a caged animal. How could she not when all this while she had shocked even herself by her actions? This had to stop. Already there was one missing night that had taken more of her than she would ever have imagined.

"Ye-yesss. That's the reason why I attended this wedding in the first place. Marg is aware that I'm giving much thought to the marriage institution, but what she doesn't know is that I need a husband fast. Like as soon as possible. Remember I did mention that my reasons weren't in any way noble."

Innu cringed at the way Bill's eyes turned from soft and passionate to cold in an instant. Even though sitting further away, she had felt the heated, probing gaze on her skin and resisted the pull to go back into the arms and have the sense that she belonged there for good. No—they were never happy ever after. This was just pure lust. His eyes now narrowed on her, suspicion lurking behind with a hint of fury that might culminate to full blown.

"If I am not married by the time I reach thirty five, which is in a month's time, I risk forfeiting my inheritance. Since I am not good at long term relationships—a temporary solution to my problem is all that I seek." Why was she explaining all this to him? It was a yes or no session here. Do you want to be my temporary husband? Yes or no.

Not this yammering and jabbering over her not being this kind of girl. She has never had to answer to anyone how her relationships went, including answering to the so-called men.

Bill folded his arms on his broad chest and quietly asked. "What about us?"

Her mouth went dry. She licked her lips. She nearly said, there is no us here, but Bill's hard expression warned her more than words would. By the way, why was he being alpha male on her, like he had the right? All soft one minute and next intimidating like hell.

"What about?"

"You know what I mean."

"Oh honey, lust. I have been there and done that. This will eventually run its course and pass," she lightly said and wished she hadn't. Bill's anger with Fletcher should have warned her enough. Guess she was a sucker for such punishment.

The gasket went off and Innu found herself huddling deeper into the seat like she would sink and vanish into it. Bill swore. Oh he definitely had a lot to say. Lucky for her, he didn't make a move towards her or she would have been clearly quivering in fear from head to toe.

Angry Bill was a formidable foe and apparently not only was she able to flip his protective, gentle and soothing button, and calm him down with her hand on his heart and her voice, she could also raise his temper quickly to a boiling point by just the flick of that silly tongue of hers.

He glared at her before he picked up his jacket from the bed and wore it.

"Umh, what are you doing?"

"Leaving."

She abruptly stood up from the chair and walked up to him. "But we are not done."

"Young missy, we are done." He said it with finality that left her itching to scratch off the self assured look he wore, in that she would listen to him and it would end there. He had another thing coming if he thought so. She had dealt with his kind before.

" I wonder what kind of a family you come from, that would request that of you and you go ahead with it. Especially considering the little incident that happened on the balcony. If you were my daughter and such a thought had passed your mind, instead of encouraging you like your family is doing...I would spank your bum hard for even thinking that. With that pretty mouth of yours you declare to my family that you love me and in that same breath explain it away that it was the lust talking."

"How do you want me to explain it as Bill? Huh," she cut in.

"Innoncencia Lockwood," he bellowed her name. Well she wasn't in the mood to be intimidated.

"Love at first sight, is that it. Honey come back to earth. There is nothing like that. By the way, number one, I am not your daughter. So you do not need to worry about me. Number two, don't act as if a while ago you weren't ready to throw me onto the bed, so a temporary agreement isn't that far fetched. Number three, if you find the thought of getting married to me that loathsome, I'm the one leaving this room to find another man for this task, not you."

Bill grabbed her hand, stopping her from that dash she had been about to make out of there. He turned her around and shook her shoulders hard.

"Who says I find the thought of being married to you loathsome?"

She yelped when he shook her, but nonetheless for some reason knew he wouldn't hurt her.

"It's no big deal." Her voice was now shaking with emotions she wasn't ready to confront. "A marriage of convenience is all I want, then after a year we go our separate ways. Simple."

"Marriage is for life dammit. Don't you get it?"

Innu shut her eyes. She had hit the snag. She and Bill were on totally two different levels, and to think Marg had warned her about it.

"I have been a fool. You know for some reason I thought this was different."

"Welcome to the real world Bill. By the way, in case you missed the memo, there is nothing like love at first sight," she repeated again.

Bill threateningly growled at her and she squarely looked him in the eyes, not backing down to admit to his hogwash that there was something more between them that had passed in the few hours they had met. She stared at the heaving broad chest, no longer able to brow beat the angry glare. He exclaimed, grabbed her hand and crushed her with his broad chest as his lips with one fluid motion took her in a kiss that had her tightly holding onto him.

The quivers started anew, that slow burn in her tummy moving down to her pelvis. The achy, needy feeling of wanting to be possessed, getting more urgent.

All she needed was to take a few tiny little steps back to that huge bed before she let him have his way with her. She knew if that happened. Soon enough he would be out of her system and she would move on with her life.

Don't forget the three years of abstinence, her mind mocked her.

Her hormones took charge, shutting down the voice in her mind with their joyful jumping to being reawakened again, as Innu reached for his buttons.

The sickening fear and dread of intimacy having vanished like it was never there. The long stretched carpet of three years, rolled up into nothing but wind in the air.

She whimpered softly, rocking her hips against him, and sank her teeth into his lip as Bill took her mouth hungrily.

"Lust," he mumbled and kissed her neck then lightly bit into it, eliciting a moan from her.

"Lust," he muttered again then took her earlobe into his warm moist mouth.

Oh my, this was crazy. He swiftly picked her up like she weighed nothing, and she wound her legs around his waist, that sense again of having done this before with him setting in.

Bill groaned, lowering Innu onto the bed as he hungrily kissed her and she emitted those little moans of delight, giving as much as she got, the kissing, and the touching. The strappy heels were yanked off so quickly from her feet before her little strappy top was unzipped and discarded in like manner. He turned her around to place more moist sweet kisses over the lacy sexy lingerie before he totally removed the bra.

How could she explain this away as lust? People didn't naturally fit like this. There was always an awkwardness at the start of things, but here they were, her touching the spots she knew so well would make him go crazy and him doing the same.

For a second, he thought maybe they were two of her kind, maybe she had a twin sister that has always been hidden from his little sis, because apart from her body being somehow a bit more fuller, hips wider and breasts larger than three years back, she still tasted so sweet when they kissed, and the long legs trailing on his hard ones still made him want to discard the remaining clothes they still had on before she could wrap her legs around him fully.

"Bill please," she moaned, wriggling her hips and reaching out to him, having unclasped the belt and opened the zip. She stroked him with her manicured nails and had him most probably swearing the roof off.

"Make love to me Bill," she whimpered breathlessly after yet another one of their wondrous passionate kisses.

That seemed to shutter the haze of passion that she had somehow weaved around him. He abruptly pulled away from her and scrambled from bed, like one caught in the act with someone's wife.

No, this wasn't happening again. Once was a mistake. This—he will be an utter fool. She had proven to him once before that he was like Fletcher in all ways, led by the waist and without a thought of the consequences.

"You know what Innu, you are right." He pulled back his pants and buttoned his shirt, his fingers barely cooperating.

"There is nothing like love at first sight, and at the same time I don't wish to marry a woman who is willing to sell herself short for an inheritance that will surely be spent in the same way it arrived. Especially one who appears to forget who she is at the drop of a hat."

She sharply inhaled, surprise setting in her eyes that had been filled with desire and beckoning him on. He knew that little speech could have had more punch if he wasn't acting like a green horn about to spill his beans by the sight of her.

"Bill, come back here."

Ya. That's her alright. She threw a pillow at him and he ducked, fleeing from his room like she might force herself on him if he didn't do so.

That's why she was his sister's best friend after all. They were both crazy.

The sound of the door as Bill fled the room had Innu throwing another pillow at the door. How could he do that? She screamed.

One moment, she was in the throes of passion and next he spews out that hogwash and leaves her hanging like this. She screamed again in sexual frustration. Of all things. How could he be so mean?

She slumped back on the bed, a few tears trickled on the side and she found herself laughing at herself that she could be weeping over a man she barely knew having run out on her. Wait until Marg finds out about it. She lightly ran her finger on the scar, funny that hadn't bothered Bill or he simply hadn't noticed. Another ache again this time of pain set in the pit of her stomach. How could she live and be happy like nothing has ever happened. This time, tears of sorrow washed over her as she curled in a ball and wept.

A knock sounded on the door that had her scrambling from the bed, reaching out for the tissue and wiping the tears away. There was no use in growing Margaret brother's head and ego in that she had been weeping over him. She reached out for a robe on the mobile rack, donned it on and went to answer the door.

Her mood plummeted to an even lower place than the floor when she opened the door and found a waiter in the midst of searching for his key card. "I didn't order any food," she snapped.

The waiter smiled at her. "Bill said you would tell me that, but to still leave the food behind." He pushed the mobile trolley into the room, smiled at her again before he left.

Bill said this, Bill said that.

She clutched at her tummy when it growled at the whiff of the food. Opening one dish, she nearly salivated. Smoked salmon, her favorite. A little bite wouldn't hurt right. Besides, she barely ate dinner. She added a few things, closed the dishes and walked over to the bed. She continued to look at the framed pictures on the side of the bed. Bill surely loved to take pictures. He was a traveler too. Duh, her mind mocked. Pilot. One particular photo drew her eyes to it. Bill was in a fancy bar, grinning from ear to ear.

She stared behind him and froze. Squinted her eyes thinking it was impossible, that it was someone else. Behind Bill, further away but still able to be captured by the camera, was a woman dressed in an Agatha Ross metallic short dress and Rene Caovilla Chandelier stiletto sandals. She knew that outfit perfectly well, since the last time she had laid her eyes on it was when she threw it in the back of her closet at home because it was a painful reminder of how far she had fallen. She knew those unique bar-stools too, a confirmation that the lady behind Bill was definitely her.

This was the place she and her family celebrated her 32nd birthday. This was the place where Dwayne, her step brother, proposed to Mia. The place where Nora, her step mother was quick to point out that she knew about Innu and Dwayne's relationship all along before she had added, your father's wealth is preferable to him than your love. Oh hell.

CHAPTER 5

"Fancy seeing you here, I thought you had a lot of things to discuss with Innu," Garret said as he sat on the vacant stool in the bar. He ordered his drink before he turned to Bill.

Bill shook his head and took a sip of his drink. He had been slowly nursing one since he left Innu in his room. That woman made him so angry, not forgetting the other part. He stopped to think like a reasonable man around her.

"I've nothing to talk about with her. We are done. She made her choice and I made mine, so I figure by the time I return to the room, she will be gone."

Liar, his mind mocked.

"I gather you found out about the inheritance."

His head snapped up.

Garret shrugged. "Marg thought Innu was acting mighty suspicious after she heard about her intervention in the restaurant, so she went through her stuff and came upon it."

"She has more sense than me."

Garret laughed. Bill swirled his drink around then took a gulp. He slowly said after, "Have you ever experienced something so bizarre to the point you thought, maybe you had imagined it."

Garret nodded. "Every time."

Bill laughed. How could he not when he was married to his little sister.

"Remember three years back when I budged into your house, wanting to strangle you for making me go through that chaste phase."

"Wait, you wanted to strangle me."

79

Bill shook his head in exasperation. "That's beside the point. I had met Innu at the bar the previous night."

Garret stared at him for a moment. Something in Bill's expression told him more since his eyes widened and he released a groan. "Tell me you didn't. Please tell me you didn't."

Bill shrugged his shoulders.

"But you both acted like you had never met before." Despair laced his voice and Bill couldn't help but laugh, even though it sounded hollow to his ears.

"She did the flash thing I gather."

Bill slowly nodded.

Garret shook his head. "How does she do it? Pretend like she doesn't recall."

"We were both drunk."

Garret snorted.

"I mean the bottom of a barrel kind of drunk. Then Elle happened."

"What. Wait a minute. You had cuts and bruises. Were they from the two women? If I remember correctly Elle was always crazy about you and would scratch any woman who came into your radius."

Bill shut his eyes and slowly opened them. "You know what. Forget it."

"For a guy who used to be vocal, you are tight-lipped about everything nowadays. Does Marg know about you and her best friend?"

Bill shook his head.

"A little information here. Something other than you slept with Innu, she appears to not recognize you like she pretends with every freaking guy she has been with and Elle happened. Did the Fletcher genes overpower you?"

Bill glared at him and Garret raised his arms in defeat. "Fine. I am not going to prod. We are men. Go screw someone else then to get over your mess. Apparently you do that a lot. Even though I showed you the best way, prayer."

Bill reluctantly laughed. Garret could be something else at times.

"I haven't screwed anyone by the way since that time. Prayer has been going mightily well, and I am quite enjoying being a man of faith," he said.

"But."

"I think my head has shifted."

Garret burst out laughing. "That bad. You can't think around Innu..like seriously."

Bill slowly nodded. He was being damned serious here and Garret was laughing.

"Ok, let's move to a safer topic. Her birthday is next month. By the way, it's a sizable amount that she will receive immediately. Not the whole lot but a quarter of it. If she stays with the man for a year then it doubles, by the end of four years she will be having the whole of it in her grasp."

"Geez Henderson, is that even a safe topic?"

Garret chuckled in glee. "I am trying here Bill. I mean you and Innu. What could be a worse combination than that? If Marg hears about this, she is going to strap Innu on the couch or bed for life."

"Tell me about it," Bill mumbled and gulped down his drink.

"Hey," Garret said. "On a serious note. This is the solution to your problem. Help her out and you help yourself out. This might be the real deal too, since Leo couldn't help but holler to us when Marg was ranting over unfeeling, uncouth Aaron Fletcher, and how he appears to always drag us into every family war, Bill has been tamed. Bill has been tamed. That's what he kept on hollering. A mere touch on the heart and the anger just fled."

Bill laughed at the description.

"You will regret it later if you don't take the leap."

"Tell me about it," Bill repeated again. He already regretted it. He had a woman whose attention span was less than a toddlers.

He opened his mouth to reveal more than he had, but decided not to. He took a sip of his drink instead and thought of ruffling up his friend with the other problem at hand. His fried brain sockets. With the marriage one sorted out, which has always been inevitable. He thought of her words again. *Temporary.* She had to be joshing. He wasn't going to be that. Over his dead body.

Already three years had passed without her, he yearned for her with his being, while apparently she had done nothing of that sort and turned up for Cliff's wedding with that blank look like she didn't know him.

Harsh and cold. That's what it was.

"There is still that issue of my head change."

Garret grinned. "I suggest you make use of the cold showers."

Bill grinned back. "The cold showers would have worked if I didn't know her. Remember. The little spots to touch and make her moan, grind her hips..."

"Whoa please don't." Garret interrupted him. "I get your point."

Bill sniggered.

"I'm still surprised you managed to get out of the room with your clothes still on your back."

Bill shook his head. Garret wasn't aware that it was barely. One look in the mirror in the corridor had shown him that his buttons weren't in their proper holes, his belt was about to slip off and not to forget the lipstick. Innu surely loved it. Garret finished his drink then he stood up and patted him on the shoulder. "Separate rooms. Reserve one now Bill, or you end up a notch again on her bedpost. I know that look. For the love of God don't touch her the way you Fletchers have been taught. Marg had me muddle headed like a dimwit. Good for us, she was the only woman on my radar. With you it might backfire since

Innu loves to try out new things so she will look for the person who made her feel that way."

Bill swore and Garret had the audacity to grin at him before he walked out of the bar.

Marg was to blame for this. If he hadn't realized who Innu was on that fateful day in the bar, he wouldn't have entertained her and he wouldn't be in the mess that he found himself in.

He settled the bill and contemplated on taking Garret's advice for once. He groaned.

"BILL!" MARG SHRIEKED over the phone as he hung up on her. He chuckled softly. She'd called him while he was leaving the bar. Drama, this is what his life had come to, in a mere eight hours. After Garret left, he was ready to call it a night but decided to sit back for a while before he headed to his room.

Like Garret had known Bill would decide to brave the lair, Donny the hotel receptionist approached him and informed him that a room was reserved for him.

Henderson of course. How could he not bloody give out a room since this was his hotel after all?

He groaned. Looks like Garret didn't trust him to be left to his own devices.

He slowly slid the door open then softly shut it behind him, pressing his head while he groaned again. This was a mistake but he had to check up on her before he retired to his own room. Marg had thrown another bombshell on him just a while ago. It was past midnight now and the wedding was soon approaching, only a few hours left.

He longed to start his day anew, to respond differently from how he had responded when he first laid his eyes on Innu. He also wished she hadn't stood in his path when Fletcher was insulting him as he usually did at every opportunity. If she hadn't, then at least he wouldn't be feeling this dread that he would brace himself over and over again at Cliff's wedding from the comments that Fletcher was likely to hail at him; including pointing out to the fact that Innu couldn't possibly love him.

He turned and nearly screamed. Or he did manage a squeak, since Innu was holding a torch to her face, standing next to him in the dark room.

"Geez, you scared me." He flicked on the light and wished he hadn't, because as soon as the light flooded in the room he noticed two things immediately. An agitated looking woman, minus her clothes, dressed in the red sexy lingerie he had partly removed before, waving a photo in one hand and the torch in the other.

Oh hell.

She was speaking fast, words incoherent, the incoherence explainable since his mind had zonked out and his eyes were wildly running over the sexy body, his mouth salivating over the picture that had just met him.

Pull it together Bill. Snap out of it. He told his mind, yet his body stiffened.

This woman was pretty intent on ruining him.

"What," he slowly asked when Innu shoved the photo on his chest and shifted away from him, then resumed her frantic pacing. She wasn't making sense.

Get it together Bill, he muttered again beneath his breath and inhaled deeply.

"When was that pic taken? Do you have any more of those at different angles and intervals," she asked him, her voice slurring slightly too.

Bill opened his eyes wide, suddenly becoming aware of his room for the first time. His clean, orderly man-cave had been hit by hurricane Innu. It was upside down. Frames had been moved haphazardly on the walls like she was searching for something behind them. On his bed were strewn more photos and her dinner dishes on the side of the bed, with a half eaten meal. Her tiny shorts must have been removed and left there on the floor like it was hopeless to fold them up and place them on the seat.

The top was on one of the lamp stands. Guess she hadn't bothered to remove it from there. And her shoes were now on his desk.

The drawers of his desk were opened, which explained the magnifying glass she now waved at him and pointed to the photo.

Was she a scavenger or what? How could she put his room in disarray in a mere few hours?

Order was the norm in his life. If he didn't have that, he would go crazy. There were two empty bottles, one on the bed and the other on the floor. The smell of the alcohol now took charge too.

"Innu what in the hell is going on here," he barked. Which seemed to make her freeze from her frantic movements.

"You do not know." She wailed out as he looked at her in confusion.

"Baby how would I know anything when you confuse me all the time."

She snorted at the endearment and instead marched up to him like the warrior princess ready to drag him if it came to that. She snatched the photo from him and placed the magnifying glass on it. "That lady behind you."

The fumes of the alcohol caught him straight on and had him pulling away. "Geez, did you drink a keg or what?"

She glared at him and answered. "I'm perfectly sober. One bottle is nothing. Now back to this..."she furiously pointed to the photo. Apart from the slight slur, the woman could hold her alcohol like any man considering instead of one bottle she probably assumed she had consumed, he was seeing two empty bottles of Whisky. Still the same, nothing had changed there. They had guzzled a few on her birthday too. They were like two kids who had been left to their own devices and discovered they quite enjoyed the freedom, including the needle that Innu deftly used at sewing him up.

Getting to the picture at hand in case it was pressed to his face if he refused to look at it, he saw the metallic little dress, cute heels and the long legs that had caught his fancy from the first time.

"Did we meet that night? Is that the reason why being with you feels natural? Why you have the familiar scent of sandalwood that soothes me instead of sending me shrieking like a banshee in panic. Did we hook up? Hmm. It can't be with those, no , no, no..."she shook her head. Bill threw the photo and magnifying glass onto the bed and caught hold of Innu's shoulders.

"If we had met, you would remember. Wouldn't you." He nodded his head, searching for a reaction. A slight sob escaped her lips and tears started falling down instead.

"If it had been you, then maybe now I would stop feeling guilty and I will go back to being me again." She shifted away from him, trembling hard as she tried to clasp her hands on her shoulders for warmth. Bill reached to the robe she had thrown on the bed and draped it on Innu before he drew her into his arms. "Hush love," he soothingly said. "Everything is going to be fine."

"You do not understand," she sniffled and another sob followed. He gently rubbed her back while she sobbed her heart out. It was official, he wouldn't have concluded that, but now it seemed to be a plausible explanation than any he would ever have thought, especially at the fact that Elle did admit to spiking his drink and Marg a while ago had informed him that she had found some antidepressants among Innu's things and had been trying to reach him.

Innu most probably couldn't remember what happened that night. Something must have happened afterwards too, considering she went off the grid and he couldn't find her.

It was sometime later when Bill gently carried her to the bed, shoved the pics to one side and laid her on it. She merely mumbled beneath her breath and turned to face the other side. He took the dirty dishes and started putting order in the cluttered room while his mind worked full time.

A mental breakdown isn't what he would have envisioned, especially from the happy woman he met that day. Crazy by all means, flirtatious, and surprisingly vulnerable at the same time. She had led him on from the moment his eyes ogled those long legs of hers, not embarrassed at all of what she was doing to him as they danced. Her body had molded into his naturally, as she did her little dirty dancing and blew his mind to smithereens.

When she said those damned words, *I'm so excited my boyfriend is disclosing our relationship to the family today*, well she just about froze his libido and cut the flow of blood in his veins.

How could a person who was about to make such a huge announcement be plastered on him like that.

A tease is what she was.

When she giggled and walked off from that dance floor, Bill's first instinctive thought was on how he longed to rush to her and sweep her off her feet before he locked her up for months in his room until she came back to her senses.

Since he was facing too many voices then, he did the opposite instead and decided to call it a night. His mind had protested like crazy.

"Just forget about my little matchmaking," Marg had said over the phone a while ago.

"Innu needs help."

He went down on his haunches and tenderly stroked her face.

What happened to you baby? He asked beneath his breath.

His heart went out to her. His beautiful woman, his...She stirred in her sleep. He stopped stroking her and got up before he walked out of the room and slowly shut the door behind him.

CHAPTER 6

Innu stirred in bed and yawned. She slowly opened her eyes and winced then huddled further into bed. A soft chuckle was heard before the other person in the room moved and came to stand near the bed.

"Afternoon sleepy head," the deep voice greeted.

"I hope that's not bravado that I'm detecting in your voice," she whispered and slowly opened her eyes again. Her head ached like crazy and all she wanted was relief. Bill must have noticed her discomfort because he encouraged, "shift a bit on the side," and settled next to her.

"Come on, scoot back over, do not be shy. I've seen you at your worst before." Innu let out a snort and leaned in to him. His fingers pressed on her temples and she released a sigh at the feather-like brush.

"How do you do that? This can't be the Fletcher touch. If it is, no wonder the many wives."

A deep rumble followed, with a slight rock of his body as Bill chuckled and had Innu commenting. "I gather Marg must have seen the pills by now and called you."

Bill's finger stilled from their ministration on her temple. "How do you know that?"

"You are being nice to me." It was now Bill's turn to snort. Innu chuckled and winced. He rubbed at the temple, soothing the pain away. "I've been nice to you from the moment we met girlfriend."

"Nope. We can't peg anything so far that you've done as nice. For starters, you unashamedly ogled at my legs, outrageously flirted, offered me a joint and gave me a glorious massage that had me thinking about sex and nothing else. Let's not forget the yelling matches that followed after I announced that our little attraction was lust. In a nutshell, in just a day, you, Bill Lewis made me go through the motions of an aged couple."

We are an aged couple.

Bill shifted so he made her more comfortable with her head on his lap and his spicy cologne teased her nostrils. He smelt so fresh and looked the part of one to be sampled on. Not that he would appreciate such thoughts about him. The eyes said so. They weren't heated like they would get, the pupils dilating every time desire showed in their depth. He acted like he hadn't heard that little barb over them being like an old couple but instead, silently worked on her head as she released little moans.

"Come on, spill it. What is bothering you?"

She chuckled softly. This felt so familiar. The way he was even asking her that, like he knew what was going on in her mind.

She clamped her mouth shut instead. He would not understand. Her project was what mattered. Not her sorry, messed up life.

"Let's just say mental illness runs in the family."

"Ohh my." A horrified look is what she got.

She reluctantly giggled. "With age, it appears I have that too."

"Is that the reason why you want to settle for a temporary marriage?"

She slowly nodded. "I wouldn't want to be a burden on anyone. Let alone my husband."

He frowned. Her hand drifted to the serious looking face. She touched his brow and commented. "You look old, don't frown so much."

"I can't help but age quickly with you around. Especially when you continue to lie through your teeth." She froze and scrambled from the bed like he had just scalded her with hot water.

"How could you say that?"

"I say that because yesterday I failed to see the obvious. You were avoiding men."

Innu briefly shut her eyes.

Damn Bill Lewis. Why did he have to be the observant one among the lot?

"Isn't that normal behavior? We stick to people we are familiar with."

"Yes we do, including socializing when we are on the lookout for a husband. From what Marg told me about you, you are not one to shy away from male attention. Tell me, why you enlisted Margaret's help, unless you no longer trust your judgment and what would make you feel that way?"

"Bill don't." She shifted to the wall and he advanced.

"What. What did I do? Did you sleep upon it and think deeply, on why of all people you don't appear to be intimidated in the least by me."

She scowled at him. "You're freaking infuriating, do you know that. I thought Marg was terrible with her inquisitive nature but you are worse. There is nothing to dig deep about here. And for your info, I still think it's all because of lust. This is why I am not intimidated. In fact," she blatantly looked at him. Ran her eyes on him fully and Bill paused. She was cornered on the wall and he knew it, that she had realized that too and wanted to pretend that she was brave and would take him on. He stared into her eyes, ran his finger on her arm and she quivered, then he leaned in to her. Innu shut her eyes.

"Soon," he muttered so close to her face and she turned up her lips. "I need something from you first." He straightened up and shifted away.

"What." Innu was in a daze. She opened her eyes since she hadn't received the kiss she was longing for and saw Bill standing further away instead.

What did he mean he needed something from her? There was nothing she could give him. If he knew better, he should run away from her while he still could. Like that frantic scramble he did the day before.

"You should get ready. Your dress is in the closet, Marg dropped it in the morning and your breakfast is on the side of the bed. The car will be coming soon to get us for the church." He took his jacket on the chair near the desk and walked out without a backward glance on her.

Innu slumped back on the bed, feeling breathless like she had run a marathon and shut her eyes.

She was beginning to see the fire she had jumped into. Within a day, Bill would have had her anyway he wished, including making her spill her guts out.

Her eyes snapped open, Bill's words coming to the forefront. Cliffs wedding, she looked at the alarm on the side and swore.

That went well. Bill patted his shoulder. In no time Innu will spill her guts out and they will be back to where they were meant to be, not the loopy nightmare again.

Bill patted himself again for being cool and controlled. He had fought hard to not rip that robe off her body, sink his teeth into those luscious full lips and make love to her. A sleepy looking Innu was even much more alluring than the fully alert one.

He groaned. Trouble did come in spades.

When he had woken up in the morning he had a crazy hard on which he tried to get rid off by going under a cold shower. He checked up on her, she was soundly sleeping, so he took a jog like a mad person fleeing from wolves. He came back and found her sleeping again, her belt having come off from the robe, exposing that glorious body. From the door he could see the long legs splayed on the bed and he cursed.

If temptation was meant to be that hell raising. He was doomed. Then she'd moaned, in her sleep.

He swore, went for another cold shower and came back.

How could a person sleep for that long? He mustered up the courage to pull the robe and cinch it tightly on her waist, not looking before he went downstairs for breakfast. That's how he bumped into Marg with the outfit in her hand.

"Big bro. This is for my future sis in law," she said. It seemed like Marg had accepted it during the night that there was no way Bill was backing out of Innu's life. Mental wreck or not.

"Go on up. She is still sleeping." He was walking away and almost about to break into a fast trot when she called him and had him pausing in mid stride. "What. I didn't touch her," he defensively said.

Marg narrowed her eyes. Then smiled, most probably at the glare he feigned out which seemed guilty like he had been caught with his hand in the cookie jar. "Be a good brother, a few last minute errands." He grumbled at the same time, relieved that she wasn't prodding like she was prone to. After completing the necessary task to ensure that the wedding went well without a hitch, he went back to the hotel.

It was way past noon and to his shock, Innu still slept. He took yet another shower, dressed partly in the suit that he had managed to take from the shop during his errands while he avoided his family in the process and made them stay away from Innu. It was after he had retrieved her meal, when he heard her finally stir. He walked up to her, marveling at how cute she still looked with her hair all mussed up and bulky.

Get it together Bill, he muttered. She is just a woman. It's just flesh over bones, nothing to be hotwiring your brain cells in the wrong direction over. Yah right. Telling that to his body appeared to not be working, not in the slightest. Every six seconds, his mind would zone off and his body would follow.

"Bill Lewis," a voice was heard calling him when he came out of the lift. Bill smiled. It was Justin Tate.

"I was on my way to you"

Bill nodded. They walked towards the restaurant on the side. "Did you get hold of her?"

Justin frowned. "She is not impressed and so is Bridge, considering the feat she pulled off so you and Elle reached an amicable arrangement. Why now Bill."

They were led to a table at the corner.

"I think it's finally time she talked and I listened, something that I wasn't willing to do then."

"Go figure, if I were in her shoes, I would have done the same. Your anger is hard to handle. You scared the poor girl from her wits."

Bill rolled his eyes. "If she weren't your wife's distant cousin, I wouldn't have been as lenient as I was. That girl nearly ruined me."

Justin nodded. "She said she will think about it."

Bill merely snorted. "There is nothing for Elle to think about, except to set the date, time and venue for our meeting." Bill changed the subject after saying his piece, not wanting the thought of Elle to destroy his mood for the day. He had a wedding to attend. He continued to talk with Justin over what Justin considered prime land for sale which he had hinted on. Justin Tate was a PI who also dabbled in other businesses too.

"Ok, I will get in touch with you in a weeks' time about the farm. Right now, heading back to see the family."

Bill nodded and stood up from the chair then shook Justin's hand.

"Why do you want to see him after this long Bill?" Justin still looked disturbed over this.

Bill frowned and Justin was in time to see a beautiful tall woman walk into the restaurant. She was breathtaking and reminded him of Sophie with her tall frame.

"I just need to lay my eyes on him. That's all and I will stay away like I have done for the past years."

"The separation is not good for you. He needs you and you need him," Justin mumbled.

With the smile the lady gave Bill and the wave of her hand, Justin was heard snorting and muttering, "Guess you want to bury the hatchet once and for all," before he slightly inclined his head to Innu and walked away.

Innu reached where he stood. "Who is that? A curious expression graced her features. Bill merely smiled and leaned near her ear then whispered. "You look stunning." That had her blushing to her roots and swatting his arm.

"Flatterer."

"I am serious. You see them, they are agog."

He was also agog actually. She was glowing and he almost changed the terms. Get her to bed fast then question later, except he couldn't do that to her. Her vulnerability was like a cloak as she looked around the restaurant like she couldn't believe that men could be stunned out of their senses by her beauty.

"Innu."

She looked up at him and smiled. That mischievous twinkle coming into those irresistible beautiful eyes and she held her head high.

Innu could feel the stares. She didn't feel dirty or scared by the looks, as she could also feel Bill's eyes on her. His presence did much in boosting her confidence. It had been a while since she felt that. He hadn't taken his eyes away from her. She turned and stared at him, delighting on how he had that look that appeared to single her out.

"Let's go." He motioned for her to place her arm into his crook and they walked out.

"By the way, you do not look bad, Captain Lewis."

"Thank you. I should warn you before we get into the car. Your little reprieve is over. The hoard is about to descend on you once we get to church."

Bill chuckled when Innu swore in answer. Very crude indeed, he thought as he ushered her into the car.

BILL HADN'T BEEN JOKING at all; Innu silently thought as she ducked from another family member and made a fast run to the door.

The Fletchers had indeed descended on her like vultures after the bride and groom were pronounced as man and wife. With that behind them, they didn't seem at all concerned with Cliff and Heather.

She groaned.

Her feet hurt from all the standing and her mouth was dry from all the talking she had done in an hour at the reception. Bill's mom had been hanging around her too and for a while it had felt a bit awkward. Then that awkwardness turned to sweetness as she continued to chat with her. Bill's mom loved him and was so proud of him. How she had missed her own mother then. The care she used to give her, her laughter, and how she would call her, her besty.

Teenage hood is around the corner, she once said to her before the accident. *Be careful of them boys.*

Innu blushed and said, "ma!"

"Don't you ma me," she quipped back. "I know you girls, always talking like you know much better with your friends. *We can't wait to start dating, we can't wait to do this and that.* Wait baby is what you will need to do. For the one who will do right by you."

"Is that how it was like with dad?"

Her mom shook her head. "No it wasn't." She giggled at Innu's frown. "I mean with your dad, yes it was. Just that I didn't wait for the person who would do right by me, I went after what you call, the right one. The one that I felt my heart yearned for. This heart is fickle love, you should use your mind and instincts about a person. Don't ignore the warning signs and think they will go away. When your daddy came, he had to get rid of the junk I had accumulated first from the others."

"Messy."

"Yes, messy." She had bent over to Innu and lightly kissed her on the forehead. "Do not get messy, you hear me."

How right she was. Innu should have paid more attention to her then.

"Innu."

"Huh."

Claudine laughed. "You have it bad huh."

"Bad, what."

Claudine giggled again and looked to the dance floor. That's when Innu noticed Bill dancing with one of the bridesmaids. A beautiful, petite lady who couldn't help but make a show of the fact that she was enjoying Bill's company." She giggled and drew closer to him.

"Mhm."

"No, I am not. Oh fuck it, I am now pissed."

Claudine clutched on her sides. "You never change. I remember Marg bringing you over to the house for that little catering gig so you spoke to Fletcher."

Innu widened her eyes and Claudine gave her the knowing look. Innu's breath hitched. The woman clasped her hand and winked. "Don't worry, your secret it safe with me."

Innu huffed. She was surprised Claudine could even laugh about the incident. Marg once begged that she spoke to her father over her coming back home late since she had to work. What had started as an innocent, ask the parent for permission thing, turned into something else as Fletcher produced a couple of hundred dollar bills, a key card to a hotel and he asked for her number.

She was shocked, numbed, stupefied. All those words that one can think of. He was her father's age for goodness sake and his daughter was her best friend, yet here he was, prepositioning her.

It didn't help at all that Fletcher was good looking, athletic, kept fit and looked half his age. She groaned. Gave him the number and left that place like the hounds were after her.

That was terrible. You know when you meet parents you expect them to be adults, but apparently Fletcher had missed that stage of being an adult. He was still in his teens because he was still trying to figure out relationships, love and sex.

"Do you want to dance," a deep male voice drifted through the fog that had suddenly set in.

"Pardon."

Claudine smiled encouragingly. "This is Max. We attend the same church and he is a good friend of Cliff's." Innu nodded and accepted the proffered hand. They walked to the dance floor.

"So Innu, what do you do for a living," Max asked as he pulled her into his arms. She placed her hands on his shoulders. He slid one arm on her back and she raised it slightly higher since it was lower than she was comfortable with.

He frowned but they continued to dance. "I dabble a bit here and there."

"Ok." He dropped his arm again. She looked to Claudine who was now occupied with chatting with the other women.

"Can you keep your hand higher please? I am not comfortable dancing this way."

"Why not, heard you're comfortable with all sorts of dances darling."

He winked at her, most probably thinking she would laugh. Great. Here was another one who had heard about her legendary exploits. She looked around, searching for Bill.

"He is gone."

"mhm" Her mouth suddenly went dry.

"I mean Bill; he had a little errand to run. Is it true though, are you really getting married to him."

"What's so hard to believe about that?"

She winced at the grip as Max pulled her tighter against his body. Good grief, didn't people at the wedding notice what was happening here.

"I mean everyone knows you, Innu. You can't decide on a whim to settle down just like that. If spontaneous, fun loving girls settled down, what would happen to poor sods like us hey?"

"Max, you are hurting me." She said in a whisper. She didn't want to make a scene. This was the Fletchers happy occasion.

A tap over Max's shoulder had him turning around. "What?"

Walter smiled at him. "Max, how would you feel if I informed Bill of the fact that you touched his woman?" Walt waved the phone. "Better yet, if I told all the brothers." Max hissed and dropped his hands. "I'm out of here."

Innu sagged in relief after Max left.

"I wouldn't have thought he could be that stupid," Walter said. "You okay," he looked her up with concern on her face.

She dragged in a breath and exhaled. "Thanks."

"No problem." He stretched his hand for the dance since they were still on the dance floor. Innu hesitated.

"Don't worry; I'm not stupid like him. Bill will kill me if I ever tried anything funny with you."

Innu nervously chuckled and nodded. She still couldn't believe that Walter had come to her rescue. When did she last see him? Right, the day she was meant to sit for her finals.

She looked at him. So many changes on his face over the years. Well they had both grown up.

"How are you here at this wedding?"

Walt slightly frowned then laughed. "Don't tell me you have been living underneath a rock to not be aware."

"Aware of what?" She blankly stared at him.

"Have you met Gordon's wife?"

Innu thought about the women she had met, particularly Gordon's. She had the hourglass shape and easy smile that would quickly win anyone over. A shy woman too, like she wasn't used to having the spotlight on her.

Innu had assumed Gordon married a celeb of some sort, singer like him or actress, yet that beautiful woman hadn't fit into any of the categories.

Walter turned her around and now she looked at the same woman who seemed so familiar but at the same time she couldn't place where she knew her from. She was dancing with her husband and looking adoringly at him.

Wait a minute. Wasn't Gordon meant to be stumbling around by the way, pants down and screaming like crazy because he was drunk? Instead a sober man danced with his woman and leaned in to say something to her that had her giggling.

"You're stunned right," Walter commented. "He pretends to be drunk to just piss her off."

Innu giggled. Weird things surely happened in the world.

"Still not a clue about that lady."

Innu shook her head.

"Her name starts with a B."

Innu swore.

Walter laughed. "You still haven't stopped swearing."

"No, that can't be Beauty. Wasn't she training to be a nun?"

Walter nodded. "She was."

"How did she become Gordon's wife?"

"The usual way, he married her and put a ring on her finger."

"I didn't mean it that way." She pinched him. She was still stunned. Beauty of all things was married to Gordon!

"Want to take a breather," Walter asked when their dance ended. She bit her lower lip. She felt safer in here compared to outside, even though for a while she hadn't felt safe here either.

She took a glance around the hall again. Where was Marg? She hadn't seen her for sometime apart from getting a few of those cold stares across the aisle. She knew it. Marg was still angry about her, not disclosing to her what she was actually going through.

How she needed Bill by her side.

Walter at least didn't make her nervous like that man had done. She had thought she would pass out as he continued with his little speech and drawing her closer than appropriate.

"I just want to catch up and I will not do so, amidst this din. Besides, I respect Bill and am a wee bit afraid of him."

Innu giggled. Who wouldn't be. Bill could be a formidable foe, considering Godfrey and Leo struggled yesterday to keep him in check. He was about to succeed in shaking them off before she got in his path.

"Fine, just keep a bottle of ice cold water for me. I will be there in a jiffy."

Walter smiled and winked before he left the room and other Fletchers rushed to her. To her relief it was the women.

She breathed in the cool fresh air and removed her high heeled sandals then she padded with her feet on the green cool grass. Good, at least no one was out here. Everyone was in the mansion, having fun. She walked further away and grabbed a bottle of water that was in the bucket of ice, then walked to the man seated on the bench.

"Thanks. I needed this." She said, smiled at him and opened the bottle before she gulped it down.

"I was beginning to think that you are not coming." Walter said with a smile.

"You were always a good spot Walt. That's why I am here." She sat on the bench next to him, placing the shoes in the middle and sighed. "This is heaven."

Walter chuckled softly on the side. Innu still couldn't believe that Walt was now related to Marg.

"I still can't believe that was Beauty I saw in-there. Doesn't she like, have a twin." she asked.

Walter chuckled, "My family was shocked too like the way you are, and considering they were beginning to accept her calling and that there was now a nun in the family. They had always assumed that it would be me heading off to the seminary and becoming a priest. When the scandal happened, they nearly disowned her."

Innu laughed and shifted the focus off his sister to him. "So how have you been Walt, like really?"

"Good." He took a sip of his wine and continued. "I have a wife and three girls now."

"You see, you wouldn't have had that with me."

"You think so."

"I definitely do. I would have run off and left you to struggle with the children while I partied like crazy. Glad I left before things got serious."

"You still sell yourself short Innu. Don't do that."

She giggled. Nothing had changed there. They sat for a while, chatting like the old friends they were before she stood up from the bench and decided to head back inside to look for her new partner who had disappeared on her. She felt neglected. How could he do that when she needed him this way?

What is wrong with you? Her mind mocked.

Lust or no lust, one fact remained. She was beginning to rely on Bill like a second limb, all because she didn't feel the dread and trepidation around him.

No matter how hard he shook her, she still didn't have the jitters. It was now dark and the lights in the backyard glowed. A few of the guests had started leaving, while the music boomed from the hall and shouts could be heard.

She was happy at the fact that Walt looked great. Their breakup hadn't affected him in any way.

Walt stood up too. "It has been nice seeing you Innu." He hugged her. She froze slightly but her mind registered that he was harmless, she had danced, chatted with him and he was safe, so she hugged him back.

He kissed her on the cheek.

"Get your hands off her."

Walter pulled away, slightly shifted but still held Innu by the waist. He looked at Bill and smiled.

"She is still a good sport, you know. If you hadn't interrupted us, in a few minutes we would have gotten it on."

"Walter!" Innu exclaimed and tried to move from the hold that had turned into a vice grip. That was a bad joke and Walter must have realized that Bill thought he had given his woman a hard snog instead of the kiss on the cheek. Even though the lights were bright enough to blind the dead, apparently Bill was thinking of murder at that point in time. Walter stiffened at the look and inhaled sharply. "Look man, it was a joke."

"Innu, come here." Bill commanded instead. He looked at Walter again and the younger man nervously chuckled and instantly slipped his hand away from the waist.

"Chill Fletcher, like I said, it was a bad joke. Just gave Innu a perk on the cheek."

"Your wife is looking for you," Bill told him. Walter looked at her and whispered. "Will you be okay or should I stay? With the way he is glaring at me, I might turn into minced meat but what the heck."

Innu smothered a laugh with a cough. A dark brow rose from the formidable man in front of them.

"It's ok, we did nothing wrong. You can go. Give my love to your wife and daughters."

Walter stared at her face and nodded for one last time and he walked away. Bill looked at her from head to toe. She shuffled on her feet and remembered her shoes were still on the bench.

He turned around and walked away, just like that, leaving her without uttering a word.

She grabbed for her shoes and ran to him. She was able to reach him when he was opening the door to the car.

"Bill, I can explain. It's not what you're thinking. Walter is an old friend of mine, and the kiss was on the cheek."

She slid between him and the door.

"Innu, get out of my way." He said it so softly but somehow she knew it was a threat. A picture of the chair being flipped like nothing at dinner yesterday drifted in her mind.

"I am not getting out of your path until you tell me that you understand what I just said."

She panted softly, trying to catch her breath from that little run.

Bill looked at the heaving chest, the little breaths she was taking and nearly groaned. She would surely kill him. He was furious at the scene he had just witnessed a while ago and wasn't in the mood to speak, because he knew he would say the wrong thing. And to think he had stayed away so he didn't send her panicking by what he was actually feeling.

Until he figured out why she had the panic attacks he couldn't properly treat her the way he wanted. Egg shells is what he was walking on and Marg had warned him over that.

"Innu," he threateningly barked. She slightly flinched but stood firm. Then he moved. Cradling her head and giving her the kiss that her pouting mouth appeared to be asking for. It was a hard kiss to punish. To inflict the same pain that he felt in his heart. How could she be so clueless? So flippant over everything, he thought as he ran his hands over that seductive supple body. Considering she once told him of Walt too. That picture had been a cozy one no matter how hard they both had denied it.

What had started as a kiss to punish turned to a gentle one instead as Innu opened up to him, so sweet and innocent like a while ago she hadn't been making out with another.

Please trust me, like I trust you in that you will never take your anger out on me, that's what her response seemed to imply. Indeed, how could he take out his anger when she responded in such a loving manner to his punishment and turned their lovemaking into not just the physical aspect but she touched his soul, knocking him down in a second? She wrapped her arms around his neck and drew closer to him.

It was like the three years of separation hadn't happened at all, as he too drew closer and she swayed in his arms, her hands lovingly running on his chest and her sweet mouth, opening up to the passionate kiss.

What he longed for now more than anything else was to touch and brand her again, remind her of what they had felt that night. He should have taken her yesterday and not tried to be a gentleman.

Innu moaned at the hungry kisses that Bill was giving her. Already her body was on heat. How could it not be when she wanted him more and more while he held himself back?

She felt herself being slightly lifted before Bill pulled away and did something that shocked her. Turned around, got into the car and the driver drove off. She was left standing stunned on that pavement while she tried to catch her breath over that wondrous kiss.

Marg rushed over to her with concern in her eyes.

"Did...did you see that." Innu pointed at the car. Marg pulled her into another one that drew to where they stood.

"Wait, what is going on," she asked once she was seated and Marg looked at her with displeasure.

She was relieved that Marg was now here in the confines of the car, despite the disapproval in her eyes. At least she acknowledged her as compared to the cold shoulder she had been receiving from her throughout the wedding. If it hadn't been for that and the fact that Cathy left early for home after she complained of her back, she wouldn't have felt alien around Margaret's relatives as they came over to congratulate her and she wouldn't have latched onto a friendly familiar face in the house and met Walter outside, twenty minutes later.

"What were you thinking?" Marg furiously asked.

"What was I thinking where? What are you talking about?"

Marg snorted. "We have a distraught wife who saw you and Walter kissing."

"huh?"

Marg rolled her eyes in exasperation. "Garret is calming Thelma as we speak. She could have caused a scene at the wedding you know, if not for Garret who spotted her distraught face when she got back into the hall and approached her. How could you throw yourself at a married man when everyone knows that you are involved with Bill for that matter?"

"No, no...Wait a minute. I hope you didn't just say that and I am dreaming. Me throw myself at Walter. He kissed me on the freaking cheek. He is my friend and I would never throw myself on him."

"Ya right, which explains Bill's abrupt departure from his brother's reception."

"I had nothing to do with that."

Marg folded her arms and looked outside the window. Innu's' heart and tummy still fluttered with nervous energy. What had taken place had happened so fast that her mind was still failing to grasp at it. How could everyone assume that she had been kissing with Walter like crazy, when the only person she wanted to kiss to her heart's content was Bill?

"Promiscuous bitch, flirt, heartbreaker," Marg muttered beneath her breath.

Innu's heartbeat tripled and she hissed. "Take those words back."

"Why should I, are they now too hard for you to swallow."

Innu had just had enough. Her friend could be a judgmental bitch at times. She always assumed the worst. No wonder she couldn't confide in her. She lunged for Marg, grabbing her hair on the head.

The driver bellowed at them, stopped the car and got out of it, seeing none of them listened to him but screams and curses followed, and the hair pulling continued. The fight went on for a few more minutes before Innu and Marg slumped on the seat and they both broke down into sobs. They reached out for each other in a hug.

"You are terrible, you know that." Innu said.

"You too are terrible. When did you start being emotional? Look at you, crying like a girl."

They both laughed as they wiped each other's faces from the tears.

"Did I hurt the baby with our scuffle?" Marg giggled and froze before she yelled. "You know."

Innu rolled her eyes and went on to wipe off what remained of the tears. "I know a pregnant woman when I see one. No matter how hard you try to hide it. The baggy clothes were a giveaway. And that dress." She whistled. Marg's baby bump was beginning to show.

"I wasn't ready to share the great news with family and friends, in the fear that something bad will happen again."

Innu nodded in understanding. Seven months ago when the general kicked her out of the apartment and Marg traveled to Prospect Ville to be with her. They looked for suitable accommodation and Innu was whining at the deplorable conditions the apartments were in. It must have been the stress and heat, including the sunny looking picture of a girl painted on the wall in one of the apartments that had Marg finally giving in to the grief and yelling at Innu.

"You ungrateful bitch, stop living in your own little world and realize that life is not pretty. You whine over your dad's money which you carelessly splashed around with your frivolous lifestyle and the fact that he is forcing you to come back home. Did you ever think about those who never had a father's love that you so bluntly throw back into his face?"

Innu was stunned at the vehemence of the tiny woman in that room as she stood near the wall and panted hard from her little outburst. "Marg what's wrong." A question she asked after a stunned, prolonged silence. "I lost her, I lost my baby." Marg replied in an anguished voice, pointed on the wall before she crumbled down and wept.

Innu rushed to her side and engulfed her in a hug. Innu found out while they both cried together that Marg had miscarried two weeks ago. Marg was right. She'd been concentrating on her family drama that she never saw the strain on Margaret's face when she came to her rescue. She did not even ask about how she was doing and how her pregnancy was coming along.

"When are you due?" Innu asked her.

"I made it past the first trimester without a hitch. By God's grace, if everything goes accordingly in five months' time."

Innu nodded and hugged her. "Congratulations. I am happy for you."

Marg sniffled. "I am scared."

"I know sweetie."

"Just like you're probably scared about something."

"Now when did we go there?" Innu vehemently protested and tried to pull away. Marg held on fast to her.

"It's ok Innu. You should've told me about the antidepressants you're taking. There's no need for you to always be strong. Life does get hard at times even to the best of us."

"Marg, I do not want to talk about this."

Marg shook her head. "We should. For a full year I didn't hear from you. People turn thirty two and start living life like they isn't a tomorrow, but you turned thirty two and disappeared from the face of the earth. I was worried sick, you know. When you finally got in touch, you didn't want to meet up. The day when I finally met you, your dad had locked you out from the apartment. I was a mess...and didn't think about the dark circles below your eyes and how much weight you had lost. That something was eating you up from the inside."

"Marg please." Innu clutched at her heart. Marg touched the hand that was on her heart in comfort. "It's okay. I am sorry for pushing it. I worry about you, that's all."

She slid the window open and hollered to Fred the driver. "You can drive us home now. Thanks for your patience." The old driver snorted as he came over to the car. Innu grasped hard on Marg's hand. "I am terrible Marg," she whispered.

"It's okay. Don't force it if you do not want to talk about it."

She shook her head and a slight tremor passed through her body as Marg clasped her hand in comfort.

"At one point my truth will come out."

Marg rubbed her hand, and worriedly looked at her. "Don't say anything. I will always be here for you and...."

"I had a baby, in the one year I was off the grid." Innu announced so quickly, before she slumped on the seat and wept.

Marg stared at her in stunned silence at the revelation while her mind failed to process the news. It was the sound of grinding of teeth that had Marg's mind drifting back to the present as she swore like her brother. Her brother had hinted that during the night Innu had a panic episode, what he had failed to mention is that it was an epileptic seizure. When Innu's body jerked, Marg hollered at the driver, commanding him to stop the car before she attended to her best friend.

CHAPTER 7

"How could you still insist on her getting married with her condition?" Bill bellowed and the General merely smiled at his agitation.

"She insists on acting normal and normal treatment is what she'll get."

Bill snorted and stood up from the chair. This was bizarre, he thought. Especially at the fact that Innu's father and grandmother appeared to be taking the whole situation calmly like there wasn't anything out of the ordinary about it. When Marg called him and informed him about Innu's episode, for a second he felt like the ground had opened up and his world was curving in.

What was she failing to tell him and everyone? And why did he think she was hiding something and that is the reason why she was now like this.

A reasonable excuse would be like she had put it; this whole thing ran in the family. Except he couldn't get the picture of the carefree woman she was before. On that one day of meeting her, he knew she was special. His mind might have been in turmoil at the time, like he was a junkie experiencing withdrawal symptoms but, just that first glance and she took his breath away. Everything on him focused on her.

Amidst the chaos, Elle throwing herself on him, her tantrums, him seeing Fletcher with a young woman fit enough to be his daughter's age at that club, Innu seemed to make total sense.

Innu's granny was watching him with glee in her eyes while Marg too wore a straight face which was slowly cracking up on the side.

"I gather you are the one who intends to marry my daughter," the general asked and he gave him an affirmative nod. They were no longer two ways about it. The farce had to be maintained, despite him and Innu having—."Did she hire you?"

Bill glared at the general and Marg was heard giggling over his reaction.

"No she didn't. I am willingly doing so to get you off her back. She is in a terrible state because of your meddling ways."

"Now Bill, Innu is in that state because she refuses to confront her past head on." Her grandmother added and glared at him. After the long look she gave him, she slowly nodded. "She made a good choice, despite the short time she was given."

Bill snorted and walked back to the seat he had vacated. Innu's family was crazier than his as far as he was concerned. The door to the room opened and a lady came in.

"Thank you my love for bringing in the refreshments, everyone needs them, considering how tense the atmosphere is." The general chuckled and the woman handed Marg the tea cup before she did the same with Bill.

Bill looked up and a shocked gasp came from the lady which had the cup and plate slipping from her hands. The resounding crush had everyone looking at them.

"Oh, Silly me. I am such a klutz these days." The woman said in a shaky voice. Bill narrowed his eyes on her.

"Honey , this is Bill and his young sister Margaret. You might remember Marg. She used to visit us when she and Innu were still in high school. Bill, this is my wife and Innu's step mother Norah."

Bill bent over to retrieve the broken pottery and watched Innu's stepmother pick some of the broken pottery too, her hands trembling. He frowned. He knew he could be formidable at times, but not to the point of scaring an old woman.

"Nice to meet you Bill," she breathlessly said and handed him another cup before she hurriedly served the rest and walked away.

"Prepare two rooms for our guests for the night."

"What." She paused at the now open door.

"Good news love, Bill is our new son in law. He will be marrying Innu soon."

Norah furtively took a glance at Bill, then quickly looked away before she gulped in a few breaths and said, "that's good. Let me get to work," then walked out of that room fast like hounds chased after her.

Bill wondered what all that was about. The surprised gasp was a signal too that Norah might be aware of something. Marg was drinking her tea and the granny too appeared to have not noticed anything out of the ordinary.

The general cleared his throat and handed him the check. "For the wedding costs."

Bill looked at him in disbelief. "I do not need your money. My intention is to get her as far away from all of you as I possibly can."

The general barked out a laugh. "Relax son. You will realize that everyone here has Innu's best interests at heart. The will was meant to propel her to move out of her shell."

"You call that move out of her shell," he disbelievingly remarked, then took a sip of the refreshing brew. The general released a sigh and placed the check on the desktop, at seeing him not reach out to it.

"Yes," he slowly said after. "You do not understand. Innu is not the same. I will give anything to have the spunky, carefree girl that she once was."

"Oh, you mean the mischievous, promiscuous daughter."

The general swore and hit hard on the table with his cane.

Bill for the first time smiled at realizing where his soon to be wife had inherited the temper from. At least the general didn't think so poorly of his daughter after all.

"My daughter has had her own share of ups and downs in relationships just like everyone else. What you call sleeping around, isn't it the same with what we men do. What's the difference?"

Bill almost hissed *she is a woman* but snapped his mouth shut. That argument was bound to make the general explode again. Besides, what was the use of revisiting the past? When he got involved with Innu, he already knew that she had her own share of ups and downs in the relationship arena.

"Would I want her to sleep around like she did before, being like a man where that part is concerned. Certainly not, but at the same time, I don't want the quivering mass of nerves she has become. One man approached her at a party she'd attended with Dwayne, do you know what happened? She shrunk and this look of terror filled her face. My daughter Bill, who could hold her own ground, shrunk away from the man like she had been struck. The terror on her face couldn't be disputed. As it turned out, she had had a few of those incidents and kept quiet about it. She wanted to be independent of us. What was I meant to do against her stubbornness? I have taken everything from her but she still insists. I have cajoled, threatened, and given her the brunt of not doing what I want but she insists on being alone. Her little project provided us with a way of making sure that we got what we want and she gets what she assumes she wants for the meantime. At least with someone around her, who will love and care about what happens to her, we would not be this worried. A year is enough for the man to see the gem she is."

Bill exhaled softly before one brow rose over something the general had said. "Wait, what proposal?"

The general swore and her nana giggled on the side like a schoolgirl.

"Son, what in the hell are you doing with my daughter if you aren't aware of the reason why she went along with this preposterous idea in the first place."

"One simple fact. I love her."

Marg choked on her tea, the general's jaw dropped open and Innu's nana was heard muttering, *this gets interesting by the minute. Those great grandchildren will be popping out sooner than I imagined.*

SOFT LIGHT RAYS FILTERED through the curtains and Innu stirred in bed. She peeked through her lashes since they appeared to be another presence with her in bed, and she was wrapped up in the presence's arms.

"Morning sleepy head." The deep voice greeted while Innu tried to make sense of why her ceiling seemed familiar to the one back home, and why hunky Bill was in bed with her.

"This is a dream, I am dreaming." She softly said, happily snuggling deeper into the warm arms and decided to test her theories. Since this was all a dream, she was free to try out what she had wanted to do before. Trailing her lips on his neck, she thought, Warm and delicious, before she lightly nipped at it. A deep throated rumble was heard and huge hands cupped her bottom, moving her on top of the hard body. She continued with her slow kisses, loving how his skin felt beneath her fingers as she caressed the strong arms, and moved her lips lower to the chest. He smelt so good and welcoming.

"Innu you better wake up fast, unless you want your family to catch us in a compromising position." The growl followed and had her opening her eyes fully.

"What!"

She scrambled from on top of Bill and his blatant arousal, and edged to the other side of the bed.

"What are you looking for in my bed?"

A delicious grin that had her heart fluttering set in Bill's features. Instead of answering her, he lazily rose from bed and reached for his shirt. Her breath gasped when she fully saw him in broad daylight. The attractive body, well sculptured and at the same time with scars here and there. She couldn't recall how she got to his side, except she heard him sharply inhale when her hand touched on one jagged scar on the side.

"What happened?" She ran her finger on it, daring too because of the reaction she was getting.

Guess their little stunt in bed a while ago had done enough, even though when she had scrambled from him, for some reason, she had thought it wasn't that. *Very funny*, her mind mocked her.

Bill turned to face her after he placed his shirt back on the chair. "Got that when I rescued a damsel in distress."

Innu looked at him in disbelief. He was wearing that mischievous grin on his face that she'd come to know so well. "Are you serious or you're just pulling my leg?"

"I am serious." He replied. "In fact, the damsel in distress is the one who patched me up. With her slender unsteady fingers since she happened to be drunk."

"Bill!" Innu swatted his arm, not taking him seriously. Like she would believe that kind of far fetched story.

"You do not believe me?"

She giggled and nodded. When he opened his mouth to regale her with the full story, Innu placed two of her fingers on his lips instead. "No need to say it, I know you were the bad boy in your days. You probably rode off into the sunset with your damsel."

"You know me so well madam."

Innu rolled her eyes, resisting the twinge of jealousy from setting in fully. "I also get why Marg thought we were a bad combination...I was like that once upon a time." She said the words so softly that he wouldn't have heard them if he wasn't paying attention to everything about her.

"And now," Bill asked, his eyes going to the pajama top she had on. Her nipples stuck through the material, showing that while they were speaking, her body had other ideas.

Innu inhaled sharply at the intense look directed on her chest, then slowly raised her arms so she hugged her chest. Bill held her arms before she achieved that goal.

"No, don't."

His eyes darkened slightly and the atmosphere in the room was suddenly charged with sexual tension.

"What about now, Innu. Are you no longer the girl that the prince would ride off into the sunset with?"

She nervously giggled. "Not by a long shot. Bet the general told you of my little episodes. I now freak out easily. Not to forget you did see me do that too. That damsel who easily trusted–that's definitely not me."

Silence followed after that as Bill stared at her and she literally felt the heat of embarrassment on her face, for having to admit that to him. Bill slowly shook his head. "No," he softly said. "You're still the same. I just think you freak out because you know that the prince and knights would be impostors."

"Really," she looked at him in disbelief.

He grinned, "Better yet, you might have met your prince and he placed you in a shell, so you never strayed."

She smacked him on his shoulder. "Ha, ha, very funny. Is the prince a wizard or what. From your description, he sounds more like the evil stepmother."

"Or he just happens to be the jealous and possessive type."

"Hmm." She remained looking into the beautiful black eyes, drawn in at the same time by them. "Where and how do I find this evil, possessive prince so he removes this curse from me."

"Do you want to get out of his shell?"

She slowly nodded and nipped at her bottom lip, her mind mocking her that she wanted to clutch at a preposterous story like that and imagine that she would ever be normal and that Bill, even though saying all this in jest, was indeed the man that she was with that fateful night. That those other men who made her feel a deep loathing over her body had not touched her.

No touch will ever wipe out the stain of those four men and make you feel clean again and yearn for intimacy. Remember them girl, how they disparagingly stared at you with lust filled eyes and went on to explain how they had taken their turns with you, her mind mocked.

Her body called her bluff because Bill stroked her cheek and she nearly purred like a kitten at his touch.

"So, how do I find the prince?"

"It's simple." Bill ran his finger on her arm and Innu softly gasped. "When he touches you, you will never freak out with him." Then Bill did just that. He drew her close, stroking her arms, then leaned in and kissed her. Possessive, demanding, slow, tender with passion banked in it as he sank into those luscious lips and his hand possessively pulled her flush against his male hardness. A low guttural sound emanated from his throat which was met with her soft whimper as she gladly drew closer and not at all fled in a panic like she was meant to.

Innu cupped his head, savoring the taste of him in her mouth, everything about Bill cocooning her up as usual and making her feel desirable, safe and content in that she would never look for another because she had found what she had been searching for all along and it was with him.

A clearing of the throat is what had them abruptly pulling away. Innu had wrapped her arms around his neck and was delighted in how sure his fingers had glided on her back, knowing where to stroke and touch and make her feel desirable from that simple act.

Even though they had pulled apart, Bill still maintained his possessive hold on her side when they turned to face Norah, who as to be expected looked not too pleased about it. She had on a long dress that swept the floor, cinched tightly with a huge belt, while the gold bangles on her wrists made their usual tinkling sound as she flapped her arms, addressing them like two teens and not the adults that they were. "Good morning Innu and Bill. I know it's normal nowadays for couples to engage in sexual activities before they wed, but please do try to refrain whilst under this roof until you're married."

Innu's jaw dropped.

"Wait—what."

Bill turned to her and hugged her before he whispered, "I will explain everything," then he kissed her again, right in front of her stepmom. An outraged snort was faintly heard as Innu forgot about her step mother's presence and enjoyed his kiss once again. He then slowly shifted away, picked up his shirt from the chair and walked towards Norah who still had that gobsmacked look over what the hell he was playing at. Bill passed her like she wasn't there and turned around, having second thoughts over what she'd said.

"By the way, soon to be mother in law," he ground out on the mother in law part and continued. "I respect Innu too much to dishonor her in the manner you just described. I've always done right by her ever since I met her, because that is what she deserves."

Norah gasped and Bill sauntered away.

Soon I will tell her, Bill thought and groaned, hoping to God that Norah will not spew her vileness on Innu and leave her feeling vulnerable. Over that self assured veneer that people saw, he knew that a vulnerable little child still lurked in there.

Tonight, he assured himself. It was time he told everyone the truth.

Innu sagged on the bed feeling breathless after his wondrous kiss. He seemed irritated to the brim too. Unlike her who couldn't fight back where her step mother was concerned, Bill didn't care about her feelings and had put her in her place. Guess he must have figured out that Norah wasn't nice like she wanted people to see her as. She suddenly felt cold and missed the comfort his whole being seemed to exude.

"I hope you didn't buy into that heroic scene just a while ago," Norah commented.

"What?" Innu shook her head to clear it from the image of how Bill had looked at her before he reached out for his shirt. The desire couldn't be disputed but it was more than that. It had been so full of love and understanding like he knew her and he loved everything that he saw.

Who was she kidding? That couldn't be it.

Norah huffed and folded her arms over her chest. "I mean that heroic scene your boyfriend just pulled. You wouldn't be taken in by that, right."

Innu abruptly stood up and started spreading her bed, in the hopes that Norah would leave the room, except the woman didn't seem to be in that much of a hurry.

"It's men like him who turn ladies into bitter-filled women at the end."

She quietly asked, stopping what she was doing. "What do you mean?"

"Snap out of it Innu. Have you forgotten who Bill is? He is a Fletcher through and through."

Her mouth compressed. "Bill is not like his father."

"Oh right, Bill is the one who plays around with other men."

"Norah!"

"What, isn't that the truth."

Innu shut her ears with her hands but Norah wrenched them away.

"Do you think if you shut your ears the truth will not sink in eventually?" She gave her a nasty smile. "What's the use of being a loving step mother to you when you always manage to disregard my words? You know that this relationship is doomed. He will be out with the men while you entertain other men too."

"Please stop." Innu clutched on her chest with a stricken look now on her face. Norah maliciously continued, disregarding her pleas. "I was there for you when you needed someone. No one is aware of the terrible person that you are. I know you Innu; you tear everything up that comes in your path. I held the fruit of how destructive you can be in my arms, the product of those four me—."

"Norah." Innu screamed her name as tears slid down her face and she slumped on the bed, clutching on her chest. Norah snapped her mouth shut. She then huffed at Innu's labored breathing and shrugged. "Do not worry and get into those panic attacks of yours so you shut out the truth about yourself. Your secret is safe with me." She winked at her and glided out of the room.

By the time Bill joined everyone for breakfast after he had freshened up, the house was full of laughter over the breakfast table. Even though no household could ever be like his, still Innu's felt cozy.

Maybe it was because of Harriet, the old family maid and Innu's nana who were regaling every one of their escapades from their youth, which might explain Innu's once upon a time naughty streak. Would he call it a once upon a time, considering her misgivings didn't apply to him? Her response to his kisses had nearly driven him insane.

Innu joined them later and Bill looked at her with concern. Her eyes didn't meet him from across the table but instead she addressed Mia, her step brother's wife and June, Jeremy's girlfriend—an Olympic gold medalist in swimming.

A brush on his arm and he turned to Marg.

"You okay."

He nodded. "Cool. Just thinking I'll have to break the news to Innu over the fact that we are getting married over the weekend."

Marg chuckled. "How could you demand that of the general though? Allow me to marry her this Saturday or I walk away. You blackmailed him."

"How was I not to do that? Do you even know your friend? A month is long enough for her to globe trot to another country, with someone else too."

Marg smacked him hard on the shoulder and giggled. Bill looked up to Innu and was in time to see her frown. He jerked his head indicating they met outside, and whispered to his sister. "Need a breather."

"You know what." She forked the bacon and took a bite. "As much as you deny being a Fletcher, you appear to take after our forefathers rather than the whole current Fletchers bandied in one. You see the woman that you want, take her in a day and ooh not to forget; you've gotten adept at the quickies too."

"Marg!"

His little sister giggled and Bill shook his head. She was a hopeless case. Day by day, Marg was turning out to be much of a Fletcher after all. Her mind surely had a one man track record. Bed.

Once he got into the corridor, a hand pulled him into what looked like a mini conference room.

He looked at the furniture, simple and elegant.

"Dad conducts most of his businesses here."

"Dad."

Innu chuckled and let go of his hand before she edged away. "The general." She took a few steps towards the windows that overlooked a magnificent back view to the mansion. This was a girl who was brought up in luxury, Bill briefly thought. The luxurious background faded away and he was only aware of her, like he has always been. She had this fragile air about her that convinced him that she needed to be protected from whatever haunted her.

The words her step mom had uttered when she was showing him the guestroom floated through. *What did she promise to give you in return? Come on Bill. Innu is known to go after men with potential. Lazz got her in the catering business. John, the doctor, made her pursue a bit of nursing on the side and not to forget the designer Drew, they both opened a clothing retail outlet which he sold after he caught Innu with one of his friends. She's a wild one.*

He cleared his throat. "We will be getting married this weekend. The whole nine yards, shindig involved, with family and friends as witnesses. You do not need to worry about anything; your nana assured me that everything will be prepared despite the short notice. My mothers are there to help you out too."

Like he had known that she would not react by jumping for joy, her shoulders slumped in dejection.

He walked to where she stood and clutched at her slender shoulders. "Hey, everything is going to be okay. We've got this."

She shut her eyes and shook her head. "I can't do this."

"Why not. Isn't this what you wanted?"

"Just cut your losses Bill. Forget I asked for your help in this. Forget it all. It will never work. I will not be able to stay with you for a year. I'm too fast. Even with our marriage temporary, I will feel like I am cheating on you when I am out with the others. I am not—," she hiccupped. "I am not a keeper."

"Who told you that? Your step mother."

She gasped and looked up at him.

"Yes love, I can tell that she has repeated that over you and you've come to believe her words about you."

"No," she turned away from Bill and the understanding she saw in his eyes.

"That is silly. I am a grown woman fully aware of what she is all about and I don't believe her words as you put it."

"Mhm."

"Yes Bill."

She could feel him draw near despite the distance she wanted to maintain and as usual welcomed the heat that appeared to emanate from him, as it circled around her. He touched her shoulder and she flinched. Bill raised his hands. "You know I will never hurt you right."

She stared at him and nodded, his beautiful eyes piercing through, searching out to uncover what secrets lurked beyond hers.

She cupped his face, wanting so much to trust him that everything will be okay. That she will not be like her mother and one day lose interest in him, forsake everything that they will have and leave it all for another man. Another excitement, another adventure without him.

"Baby I love you." Bill softly said. She shut her eyes from that beautiful dream. It couldn't be true.

How could he, when he didn't know the terrible things that she had done.

She shook her head.

"Yes, love. Don't shut me out. Look at me."

She slowly opened her eyes.

"Whatever it is that you feel you have done wrong, you can tell me, you can trust me. We will get through this together."

Fresh tears started falling.

"Stop it. Please stop it." An image of the four men drifted in her mind and she shook it away in vehemence.

"Just Stop it. Don't do this. Don't try to act like you understand me. I am a horrible person. I get it too why you would want to marry me. Just to spite Fletcher."

Bill swore.

"What. Did you think I didn't notice how much his words hurt you?"

"It's not about that Innu and you know it. I just about spilled my guts here and told you I am in love with you."

"Really," she challenged.

"What if I am to tell you that I was once involved with your father. What will happen to your love for me, hmm. What if I showed Fletcher more than the long legs that you ogle at all the time? I wrapped them around..."

"Innu!" The threat in his voice made her wary yet she was in a self destructive mode. She was tired of being her, of holding it all in. The regrets and the wrong decisions she had made over in her life.

"You loathe the very air that he breathes and yet you are willing to take his scraps."

"Innu!" Bill bellowed and slammed hard on the table. She flinched. He pulled away from her and made like one leaving. He must have decided to say his piece, because he whirled around to face her, furiously heaving with his temper barely held in check.

"You." He pointed at her. "Enough. You hear. Enough. What are you trying to do to me? Are you trying to kill me so you prove that I can't have fallen in love with you? Guess what sweetheart, I am sorry but I already did three years back. That's how bloody long I have been waiting for you to come around. To accept what happened between us. Innu we...", he shook his head and shut his mouth. What was the use of recalling their history together, seeing she didn't care, and she never cared about what happened, except to only run away from it.

Three years. He was mad to have waited that long. She was right. He should have cut his losses then.

"From the way you have been acting it reminds me of then too. I guess toying with people's emotions is what you do best. For a second, I actually thought everyone was wrong and you were misunderstood. Seeing the way you have been pushing me away means two things, either you remember our night together and it meant nothing to you, or you're too deluded to realize what you are doing."

"Bill," she softly said and made like one who wanted to touch him, the anguish in his eyes tearing up her insides.

"No Innu. Enough." He stopped her with a raised hand. Halting the few steps she had taken towards him.

"Enough right. We end it here. Right now for good," he turned away and walked out of the room, banging the door behind him.

Innu slumped on the ground, glazed eyes and empty of any emotions, a deep ache having set in at the moment. Where she would have felt relieved at finding out about her and Bill, anguish is what she felt instead. It meant that she had been with him and afterwards, those four other men. Oh God, what had she done?

The door softly opened and her grandmother walked in.

"What was that row about," she inquired.

Innu stared at her and the tears slowly started falling again. "Grandma," she whimpered and the old woman drew near and touched her face.

"I gather those great grandchildren will not be coming anytime soon then."

Innu sniffled as her grandmother wiped the tears from her face.

"What did you do chile."

"He said he loves me."

Her grandmother laughed. "That's good right. Why the argument then."

She shook her head. "He deserves to be with someone who will be good for him."

"And you think you are not."

She nodded.

Her grandmother scoffed. "I should have known that you would be the same in every way like your mother. Self destructive especially when you meet someone who loves you past the things that you feel you have done. Nonetheless you are not your mother, so do not repeat her mistakes and let a good man go from you like this."

Innu shook her head. Her nana cupped her face harder. "Yes Innu. You might fail to tell me what is going on with you, but please do speak to someone before it is too late. Once you do so, let it go Chile..let it go." She finished and hugged her.

CHAPTER 8

March, 1994

Aaron Fletcher narrowed his eyes over the outfit Bill was wearing. He was furious to have been called to the principal's office and wasn't hiding that fact from him. "What in the hell are you wearing," he softly asked, his temper in check but about to blow off if Bill made a smart remark like he usually did. Bill stood up from the chair, a tissue still on the cut lip.

"A robe."

He walked away and Fletcher swore. "Boy, I am not done talking to you." Bill hastened his pace instead of heeding to him. He didn't want anything to do with him just like Fletcher didn't want anything to do with him.

Once they were outside, Bill walked towards the gates. A yank at his arm that made him grind his teeth and his eyes smart from the excruciating pain, followed.

"Do you expect them to not call you a sissy when you dress like this?"

Bill said nothing but angrily looked at him.

What did he know anyway? What did Fletcher know about him, his mother and brother?

His mother struggled to put food on their table, was always exhausted every time since she juggled three jobs by herself. They lived in a small apartment and they had been content including with the public schools they attended, except Fletcher didn't want any of his kids to be at a public school. Private is what they were entitled to. He plucked them out from what was familiar to them, to a territory that Bill loathed with all his might.

Other kids made fun of how he talked and how he dressed. Today was the final straw. His mom made a mistake over the order of his gown for a school play. Instead of the gray one specified by the school, she must have selected pink by mistake. How could she not when she was functioning like a zombie all the time, tired and with dark rings under her eyes. The strain of keeping up with sending Bill and Denzel to a private school was getting to her more each day. While Fletcher handled the exorbitant tuition fees, everything else fell on her.

One look at the gown when it arrived and she'd broken down in heart wrenching sobs.

Bill at ten years old, found himself comforting his mom like she was the child and he the adult.

"It's okay mom. I will wear it."

"They will laugh at you. How could I make such a stupid mistake?"

Bill wiped her tears off her face.

"Don't worry. They will not."

Denzel came on over to the couch where they sat and hugged her too. He was done with preparing supper. At twelve Denzel had won a few awards for his culinary skills and tomorrow he would be going for the junior chefs' competition.

"My sweet boys." Their mother crooned, tearing up as usual and kissed them on both cheeks.

She wiped off the tears from her face and smiled at them. "Let's eat and go to bed. Tomorrow is another day." They gladly walked to the corner table in the huge room where there was a simple yet delicious meal.

After they were done, she headed to bed. Bill knew her heart ached as she walked away from them. Denzel's eyes showed the same. She would cry herself to sleep. Hoping they didn't hear her do so.

Denzel shrugged and started clearing up the table while Bill headed for the sink to start washing the dishes.

"Are you going to be fine tomorrow?" Denzel whispered concern evident in his voice.

Bill nodded. "I will be. Just do your thing and wow them at the competition."

Denzel smiled. "You bet, and enjoy the play."

Bill did enjoy the play despite the first few seconds when he got onto the stage with his pink robe. The crowd had roared in laughter but was soon won over by his acting skills. He was a king, in his own kingdom, assured and very much attuned to his role. A resounding applause followed from that beautiful performance.

It was after the show when the other boys attacked him, making fun of him and he fought back with punches. One barely managed to scratch at his lip. That's how his father was called to the principal's office.

"I am not a sissy," Bill growled and received a thump on his head.

Fletcher released a snort of disgust over that remark. "How many times have I told you to not be this outspoken. Your mom is spoiling you too much by taking you along to the hair salon. Now you are talkative like the rest of the women and you even wear pink dresses."

"Robe—," Bill corrected and Fletcher rolled his eyes.

"Where is she by the way? She was meant to be handling this, not me."

Bill curiously looked at the handsome man who appeared to be acting all clueless, when he could remember so well that his mom called him yesterday.

"Your son Denzel, remember him. He is participating in the junior chefs' competitions, so she had to be there."

Fletcher frowned and then retorted, "great, I have a cook and a cross dresser. Claudine surely churned the weirdos."

"I am not weird," Bill snapped. Fletcher raised his arm to hit him and Bill stood his ground, glaring at him like one who would return that slap on him too. Fletcher stopped before he hit him, threw back his head and laughed. "You are the fighter in the family like Leonard. That fierce look, those four boys didn't stand a chance."

Bill was taken aback. His father was complimenting him! No , he always disparagingly spoke to him. His mouth had opened in shock. As if to burst the bubble that had slowly come up, Fletcher winked.

"Hello darling."

Bill turned behind him and saw a lady in her twenties; she winked at Fletcher and commented. "Guess you are having a bonding time with your boy. He is cute." She looked at Bill and smiled. Bill snorted and walked away from them. His father was back at it, flirting with everything with two legs. No wonder his mother always cried all the time when she thought he and Denzel weren't looking.

"Wait up." Fletcher called him.

He wasn't listening but was more intent on getting to the bus stop.

"Bill, let me take you home," Fletcher said.

"I will go on my own. You go back to your busy life."

Fletcher narrowed his eyes and slowly nodded. "Fine. Leo and Godfrey are on a semester break, so we are going camping. You should pack up. I will pick you up at eight. It's time you were taught the Fletcher ways."

Bill opened his mouth to refuse.

"If you refuse, I will have to inform your mom of your suspension from school for the next two weeks and give her the hospital bill for one of the kids whose arm you broke. How could a ten year old like you break the arm of that big thirteen year old."

Fletcher looked at him in disbelief while Bill fought the urge to retort, *it's all because of you. Everyone says negative things around me, always mocking my mom on why she is involved with you. She is my world and you hurt her all the time. I have been bullied non stop because of you.* Instead he fisted his hands on the side while the man who looked so much like him, stood with the same stance too.

"Fine."

"Fine," his old man vehemently said back, before he whirled around and walked away, to the luxurious car parked nearby and drove off. Bill got into the bus and slumped on the chair, and then he cradled his face and wept.

PRESENT DAY.

"Bill," Innu said his name with a voice full of emotions. She'd done nothing but cry throughout after her talk with her grandmother. Marg left in a hurry before they could chat since Garret had called and informed her that Gail was running a fever.

Her heart sang at the fact that he'd come back. Bill was here, in her room.

"Hey," he greeted and cradled her face. She inhaled sharply from his touch. "You shouldn't cry this much. You look like a panda."

Innu swatted his arm. He smiled; even though it didn't reach his eyes and he hugged her. She wrapped her arms around his neck, dragging in his wonderful scent and letting his presence calm her. How she'd missed this. When she thought she'd cried more than enough and was spent, here she was, doing it again. Bill pulled back. "Hey, hush." He wiped off her tears with a clean hanky and lowered her back on the bed and when she was sitting, shifted away.

"Bill, I'm sorry for the things I said in the morning."

"It's okay." He briefly shut his eyes and opened them.

Please don't leave me. I need you. Don't say you've decided not to marry me, because you are my only hope and I can't do this with anyone else but you. Those are the words she longed so hard to say to him. That he be patient with her and still love her like he'd told her in the morning. Instead, the sad look that Bill gave her when he opened his eyes told her something different. This wasn't meant to come as a shock. She'd been rejected by men before, so this was nothing new. She would get past it like she'd done before.

"We are still getting married on Saturday—don't worry."

He shook his head and went on his haunches, close to her before he took her hand into his huge ones. The tears were now falling again.

"This will be temporary like you want. I'll stay out of your hair until our wedding and do the same after."

She looked up, closely peering in the deem room, the sun having set a while ago. That's when she became aware of what he was putting on. His uniform. Like she has always known, he wore it in the same manner he wore the designer suits, like it was specifically made for him.

"Are you going back to work?"

He slowly nodded. "Everything will be handled the way you want. I will see you on Saturday. Hey."

He cradled her face, she was sobbing, this time more audibly.

"Isn't this what you want Innu?"

She nearly said it. That this isn't what she wanted with him, but something real. The words couldn't come out. She couldn't confess that she too loved him. That she too felt what must have hit him and had him confessing in a few hours that he was a goner.

She wiped her face instead and nodded then looked aside so he never saw the turmoil going on in her. She heard him sigh in resignation before he stood up from his crouching position. The sound of the door closing is what made her aware that he was gone.

She lay on the bed and wept.

CHAPTER 9

2 *days before the wedding.*
Bill slowly walked up to his room. He was beyond exhausted. Just one step he would take required so much energy that he felt he no longer had it in him. For a couple of days he'd been acting like a maniac when he went back to work, including dropping the bombshell that he was retiring. It was time he set his roots. Even though his life with Innu was still not clear, he knew that his work would not give him the time he needed to woo her again. During the years, he'd made a couple of wise investments too hence he continued to fly, not because that's where he derived his livelihood from , but because he loved it.

Would his decision be an easy one to bear, he wondered, considering flying had become like second nature to him. He thought of his old gramps, the one he was named after and of how he'd admired him. Bill and Denzel would take turns from an early age to wheel him to the huge mango tree in the yard where their tiny flat was located. The big five storied building was occupied by different families from all walks of life; hence children would be always running around in those grounds, people who Bill had come to view as family. They were a small community that looked out for each other.

Bill was fascinated with his gramps stories while the other kids would jokingly point out that there was no way old Bill ever flew anything. The old man was probably no one of importance in the army like he claimed, seeing he and his family stayed in their neighborhood.

Dreams, it's all his selling us and they will come of naught. One of the boys once said, while Bill and Denzel derived strength from those dreams, since they had seen the photos to attest that their gramps wasn't a loony. He usually told them that they were capable of doing anything that they set their minds to. When his grandpa died, who had appeared to be vehement all the time about Fletcher taking his daughter despite the fact that she had two children with him, that's when Bill's life fell apart.

He was just ten years old when Fletcher decided to chip in, changing his life around like it was nothing. He changed where he and Denzel went to school and eventually removed them from the neighborhood. A health scare caused the final shift and for his mother to move into the mansion where the other wives of Fletcher stayed. For years after, Bill strived to not be weak in any way to the point his mom would be put in a vulnerable position like she was when he was diagnosed with type 1 diabetes.

He forgot his gramps words too in his quest to anger Fletcher, the man he loathed the most. He forgot the stories of hope the old man had shared with him. He forgot about the peace that Bill senior spoke of when he was in the air, marveling at the beauty and what lay beyond the surface. Above all, he forgot to dream.

Bill was twenty and in a dark place in his life after trying every daredevil act to make him feel alive and that life had something more to offer him than the misery he felt when he wasn't high on adrenaline. That was when he looked up into the sky and saw a plane, far above, and then remembered what his gramps once said when he was a kid.

He was looking into the sky and had this serene look on his face when Bill remarked. "Gramps, have you gone to your happy place again." His gramps had laughed at that before he pointed. "You see that speck up there. It's a plane." Well Bill screwed his eyes, not seeing anything while his grandpa laughed. Then he saw it. It seemed so tiny up in the sky as it passed.

"Do you know it's when you go higher, that you have a different outlook to everything below? One day when you think you can't see what's ahead, just change your standpoint and look from above. You will definitely love the view."

Bill literally took that advice then. Besides, there was nothing to keep him grounded. His mom was disappointed in him, he had had a brush with the law a couple of times and hearing her pray and blame herself for the choices he made, tore at him more.

Even though he loathed the Fletcher side of him where his libido was concerned and strove for the Lewis side of him to be in charge, self willed and in control, he was thankful because apparently he had the Fletcher intelligence too. Fletchers always strived in any field. It was so easy and effortless once he decided to take the aviation route and by the time he turned 30, he was the youngest in his team to be made captain. Now turning forty he felt it was time to be grounded.

He slid the key card to the door and opened it. Awareness that he wasn't alone in the room passed down his spine and he straightened from his tired slouch.

"Hello Bill," Innu greeted him in her sultry voice. He didn't have to flip on the lamp to know that it was her. He knew her like the back of his palm and she was the only woman that he ever sensed when she was near.

He reached out to the switch and she stopped him.

"Please don't."

"What do you want Innu," he asked her and slid his hands into his pockets instead. She drew close to him, her sweet floral scent teasing his nostrils when she reached his side, then whispered. "We need to talk."

"What about. 'Thought we said everything that needed to be said."

"No we didn't." An outline of her shaking her head could be seen from the moonlight filtering through the curtains.

She took his hand and placed it where her heart frantically beat against his palm. "You can't flip on that switch until I'm done with what I have to say. As it is—I'm scared." Her voice trembled on the last note, and there was a plea for his understanding in it, except Bill was too tired and irritable. When would she stop being a drama queen? She had plagued him daily since he left her home, a shimmer of her image always before his eyes as he tried to go about his life.

The day when she left him, he was busy trying to come to grips with Elle being in his bed, sorting out that mess, but once it settled, that was when it hit him. He had done more than sleep with his little sister's best friend on their first meeting. He'd married her and she'd run off, probably after it dawned over what she too had done.

Normal men saw a pretty face and admired her from afar when they discovered that she was not available. To top it all, vulnerability spelt trouble to them and a demand that they would never meet, so they usually skulked away from the hero worship mentality. Only a-Fletcher would rush in to save the day and think of the repercussions later. Be insatiable to the point he bound a woman to him, knowing he would do it over with someone else when they caught his fancy too. Fletchers loved pretty things and didn't let them go until they finally had them in their grasps.

He'd felt like all his forefathers mocked him since he had sworn to never be like them but would be noble like his grandpa Lewis. He'd sworn a lot of things actually, like not wanting kids too, including proudly voicing it out to Fletcher and watching him shrink in disgust when he announced to him that he was gay.

In his thinking, how would he have handled kids when he grew up without a proper father figure? The malfunction in the equipment with Innu that night had them laughing their lungs out and he had been drawn by that mischievous look that was on Innu's face and her words. *I would give anything to have your baby,* before she removed the protection as they made slow passionate love for the remainder of that night before he dozed off.

If only he had known she would slip out of his bed; he wouldn't have slept a wink then.

He had nonchalantly asked his sister about her friends during the course of the years, knowing full well that it was Innu that he searched for. Too much water had passed under the bridge, for them to act in this manner and he was tired. While she scrambled everything he had stood for to mash, she seemed well and intact.

Guess there was nothing to bind them too, seeing that equipment failure never produced anything, but apparently if it were to be believed another equipment malfunction had occurred with another woman and she wasn't lucky like Innu.

Two women had ruined him in one night. One he loved with all his might and she didn't remember him and the other that he didn't love, but he was forced to keep by his side because she had something of his.

He reached out with his hand and flipped the switch on. She covered her eyes with her arm. His eyes ran over the sexy black lingerie she was putting on. Great. As to be expected, she had resorted to messing up with his brain wiring and his body.

"Put a robe on," he commanded and shifted away from her, then sat on the bed and waited. Innu did just that. She braved a look at him. He knew he didn't look too pleased at her little stunt.

If she thought he was pissed off because of her trick and that he didn't find her attractive, she was further from the truth, since he was indeed pissed off but for the mere fact that with the way she looked, it made him want to take her to bed in that moment and forget about everything else. When he wanted to tenderly woo her to submission, she messed up his mind and brought out the Fletcher instincts instead.

"Why are you dressed like this and in my room?"

"I thought this would make you listen."

"I am not like all the other men that you managed to turn their mind to mash so they listened to you. If you want an adult conversation, you better act like one and make sure you are fully clothed while doing it."

She briefly shut her eyes and he could see the struggle and how she tried to keep from lashing out on him in the same manner he was doing to her. She clenched her hands on the side into tight fists.

"Oh. You mean the mature way you've been acting. You haven't been picking or returning any of my calls."

"I've been busy. You know some of us do work for a living and don't have trust fund monies to tide us through the years which will also be passed to the next generation."

"If you loathe what I stand for in every way, why are you marrying me?"

We are already bloody married that's why.

"You asked for my help and I am doing just that. I wouldn't want to see any of my little sister's friends doing anything stupid."

"How so noble," she snapped, rubbed her arms and fumed on the inside at Bill's tone. He was just being cruel and an ass.

What did she expect anyway, considering she'd asked for this emotionless, cold and temporary arrangement? Besides, she wasn't here to seduce him like he thought. If only his mind wasn't too wrapped around the injustice she might have or might not have done to him, he would have realized how she'd trembled when she took his hand and placed it on her chest.

How she had tried to get rid of all the layers so he noticed the scar and the not so perfect skin, which now had signs that at one point, her stomach had stretched and extended. He would have noticed too the stretch marks that she always hid with makeup on her boobs. She had carried a child and there was no point in trying to hide that anymore. She'd tried every recommended tissue oil to get rid of those but apparently her skin had other ideas. Her indiscretions couldn't be hidden anymore and those marks were proof of that.

"You know what." She abruptly turned away to grab for her clothes. "Reasoning with you is useless when you're being such a grouch, I should go."

"How do you know that I'm being a grouch?" He asked mildly. "Maybe this is my usual expression. This is how I speak to everyone. I'm not a nice person, sweetie. You can't walk over me then decide to come back in with your tail tucked between your legs and hope I will roll over for you."

"I don't expect you to roll over for me."

"What is it that you expect then? What is it that you want Innu? Mind blowing and body numbing sex that you've heard that we Fletcher's give, is that it. Do you want me to take what you are offering me, so you can talk about it with every woman ready to listen over what a stud I am, is that it."

"I'll never do that," she whispered, giving him a horrified look while he glared at her. "You know." He stood up from the bed and tugged at his tie. "Let's get it on honey. Remove those panties and come." For a second Innu was stunned as Bill unloosed his tie and reached out to unbuckle his belt. Her confession had taken a nosedive for the worst. She glared at him and watched him pull down his trousers before he stepped out of them. Such a typical man, she thought and whirled away from his stripping episode to get out of the room. She hadn't been offering him sex, but was baring her soul to him.

"One step out of that door and the wedding is off," he said softly and she froze.

She angrily turned around to face him and yelled back. "The wedding might be off where you are concerned, but I promise you that I will be walking down the aisle with someone else on Saturday."

Over my dead body.

His shoes followed before he strode to where she now stood, disbelief now having replaced the anger. He was a strong man, who towered over her, his presence shrinking the room and making her aware of the folly in coming to his room in the first place. He looked sexy too, despite the fact that he didn't have his pants on, just his jacket and shirt with his tie loosely hanging from his throat, his boxers on strong thick thighs, socks minus the shoes.

"Try me." She challenged and slightly tilted her head higher, ready to hail as much as he was willing to dish out to her.

They both stood in the middle of the room, panting heavily and looking angrily at each other, none in the mood to back down.

It happened so fast. One moment they were glaring at each other like they would both commit murder and the next they were in each other's arms, kissing like it was the last time they would ever be together. Like it was their last day on earth.

Desperation, old hurts and pains, fresh and new wounds, were all felt in the passionate kisses they gave each other. From the touches on what the other will miss out on, if ever they decided to be with another.

Innu didn't care that she was actually giving in to the offer he'd made a while ago.

She moaned as Bill hungrily kissed her and with trembling fingers she removed his jacket and unbuttoned his shirt. She became more agitated when his warm moist mouth moved to her neck and he sucked and lightly bit into her skin, while his hand on her breast teased the nipple, rubbing it till it became a hard nub. She was a quivering mess and that action made her inhale sharply before she tugged at his shirt and ripped the remaining buttons off.

He chuckled softly at her gasp over what she had done before he pulled her towards the bed.

"Your shirt." Despair marked her voice and he kissed her passionately so she didn't say anything else. A whimper instead came out from her lips when he ran his huge hands on her bottom and pulled her closer. He'd cradled her head and was making slow love to her lips, while her hands trailed now on his exposed body. Feeling the silky skin beneath her fingers and the familiar scars.

She squealed in delight when they both tumbled on the huge soft bed and her body was molded into his hard ridged one, his warm skin over hers. He shifted his hard body pressing into her as he kissed her all over her face, her neck, moist little kisses that made her long for more. She moaned since he had fully removed her bra and now sank his teeth into her breast, his moist tongue licking and nipping on the nipple while she slid her hand into his boxers and cradled him, then stroked the hard silky rod.

"Baby, the boxers," she mumbled, wiggling beneath him and wanting him to shift so she removed them completely and she finally felt him. Deep inside of her where he belonged. Her pelvis and core were on fire.

"Tired—exhaust..," then silence.

The kisses stopped. The stroking of her breasts stopped.

"Bill," she said. That's when she heard it. A soft snore and breathing that raised the hairs on her nape. His weight on her was becoming more uncomfortable, so she shifted. He mumbled something and turned away to her horror. Great. If there was one person who made her feel like an unattractive tin of pureed tomatoes, it was him. How could he fall asleep in the middle of that?

She snorted in irritation, annoyed at herself too for getting carried away. She scrambled from the bed and wished she could get a bucket of ice cold water and dump it on his head. The more time she stood there fuming, she began to take in other things too she hadn't noticed. Like the stubble on his jaw and the hair that hadn't gone through the brush for that day. In the days she had come to know him, she'd noticed that he took his grooming seriously. He was always clean shaven, his cut up-to-date—too clean for her liking and his suits impeccable and just perfect. He was one of those smart, clean guys who made a girl feel like she needed an extra scrub and to undergo the one year beauty therapy session Esther in the bible went through before she met with the king for that one night.

She sighed and retrieved the jacket on the ground and shirt and slacks, then placed them on the chair. These didn't look at all like the uniform he wore the day when he left, instead this one was a uniform on the verge of falling apart. No wonder her ripping episode had sent the buttons flying like ping-pong balls. She walked to the closet and opened it. A few designer suits lined up the rail, his uniforms and at the corner a box that was partially open. She removed it. The guy was a neat freak to a fault, she thought, seeing the packaging on his old uniforms.

Would Bill have been so distracted for the past days that he'd started putting on his old uniforms? Maybe it was to remind himself of where he came from. She opened the closet again to return the box and caught sight of two pairs of well worn trainers and faded jeans. An album was on the shelf. The box must have probably been on top of it, that's why she hadn't noticed it before. She gasped when she opened it, and pictures of Bill with his brother and mom, looking happy and in what appeared to be a hair salon, then diner and at a stall full of cosmetics. She didn't see these pics the last time she rummaged through his room.

They were of Bill in his early years. In all the pics his mom would be putting on different uniforms, while the boys appeared to be wearing the same clothes with an old man on the wheel chair on their side. The photos looked like they were taken on the same day. More pictures revealed a happy Bill, smiling up to the camera with no care in the world, the old man a constant figure in his life.

She guessed that he must have been their grandfather. She went back a few pics and realized the commonality of the clothes. In the other pics Denzel had worn those same clothes. She giggled at one where he had a pink robe on, and he was holding what looked like a plastic sword, but that twinkle she had seen in all the pics wasn't there. The old man was no longer there either.

High school pics, nothing out of place where his dressing was concerned, no longer the shabby happy kid he once was, but smartly dressed with now a broody look in place of that open smile. She frowned and remembered that Marg once pointed out that Claudine's arrival to Fletcher's home coincided with Josephine. For a few years before, Claudine for some reason had taken care of the boys on her own until one of them fell sick.

She froze. Diabetes, Marg had said. She looked to the bed, and the man was still sleeping soundly on it. To confirm that the moment his mother settled with Fletcher, Bill was no longer the same, he lost the twinkle of joy in his eyes, the photos that soon followed had the permanent frown, including the one of his high school graduation. Bill was glaring at his father who was looking into the camera, smiling broadly and oblivious to it.

What followed were now pics of him looking sauced, with his arms wrapped over guys while he either smiled or winked at them. Ones where he must have landed on the ground after paragliding, seeing the chute was behind him, outside a boxing ring with his gloves still on, outside a well beaten up car in what looked like a racing track. He would be having a few scratches too, and always a man on his side.

She shut the album in disbelief. What have you done Bill? She muttered beneath her breath and knew deep down what he must have done in his bid to hurt Fletcher. Fletcher must have been disappointed to find out that he was gay. To see his spitting image get involved with men. Fletcher might have seen what Bill wanted him to see, a rebellious son who would never conform to anything he wanted, but she saw something else instead, and remembered when he said he got hurt doing daredevil stunts. Bill also risked his life with his choice of activities, probably not caring if he died. Bill must have loathed his existence at one point in his life. She gasped at the thought, and slowly stood up from the ground where she'd sat flipping the album and walked to the bed, looking at the handsome man who slumbered in it, relaxed. He appeared to find peace in his sleep.

She realized why he'd seemed so understanding the few times he had wanted to probe into what was happening to her. They were so much alike at every possible level.

Hadn't she too fought against everyone who compared her to her mom? Her first boyfriend had hurt her so bad, that when she confronted him over seeing him with another girl after she gave him her heart, body and soul, Lazz merely laughed and said, *sweetheart, you knew this wasn't going to last. How would I trust a person whose family has a track record of infidelity? As the saying goes, like mother like daughter.*

From that time she never fully gave her heart to anyone. There was always a feeling on the edge that whatever relationship she would get into, it wouldn't last. Even though usually it was concluded that she would have cheated, it was never like that. She just moved on fast like all the men. If she was dumped or she dumped a guy, on that same day she would be having another beau. To her friends she seemed like she was fast, yet that is how she coped.

She rolled down the socks, and placed them on the side. A slight shake to his shoulder, had Bill sleeping more comfortably. She retrieved the fleece on the foot of the bed and draped it over him. He had left room enough for her to lie next to him, so she shrugged her shoulders and lay as far away from him as she possibly could.

She gasped when Bill reached out to her and pulled her close to him, covering her up with the fleece and the warmth of his body seeping into her.

She thought he must have been having a dream, pulling another woman into his embrace rather than her hence fighting it by trying to pull away, except he held her fast to him, pulled her closer than before and nuzzled her neck.

"Go to sleep love," he ordered. "I love you so much Innu that at times it hurts." She gasped at his statement except he'd drifted off to sleep again. For a second she was stunned by his words, then gave into the inevitable as she turned around to face him, lay back her head on the pillow and slowly ran her hand on his face .

She'd thought by now he would hate her. What a fool she'd been, and it was time she stopped being that, seeing that it has always been him that she'd been searching for all along, a man who understood and loved her despite her faults. She slowly shut her eyes and she too drifted off to sleep.

CHAPTER 10

Bill opened his eyes and groaned. A woman was softly humming in his room when all he wanted was to sleep forever. She chuckled when he put his arm over his eyes. "Wake up sleepy head," she ordered.

Bill opened his eyes and looked straight at Innu. His eyes widened further when he didn't see the silky long legs he'd come to associate with her.

"Sweet Jesus, you're fully dressed."

She looked at her clothes then giggled. At least he appeared to be in a joking mood today, since his first remark had actually been funny.

"Come on." She reached for his arm. "Get up. We should get moving or we will be late."

Bill narrowed his eyes suspiciously on her and she rolled her eyes. "Don't worry; I am not planning to murder you or anything."

"Yah right," he mumbled and reluctantly got out of bed before he headed for the shower.

"That went well," she mumbled, then smiled. She was feeling great actually and her day appeared to be on a great start. Bill hadn't thrown out his fiery barbs on her and he wasn't angry. Or maybe he would be, once he got out of the shower, which meant she had to scramble before he did so. She placed the note near the warm plate with his breakfast, just a few words. *Meet me downstairs* and a couple of hearts, not to forget, she kissed the note. Perfect. Operation wooing Bill was in full swing. She walked out of the room with a slight sway to her hips while she dialed the number to her dad's pilot in that they would be on their way in thirty minutes time.

Is my woman back, Bill asked himself as Innu took a couple of selfies while they were in the chopper. Or she was still being the schizophrenic

144

patient he'd come to know. He watched her fully smile into the camera, and then stick out her tongue before she zoomed the camera on him and took a couple of pics of him.

She had been in that chirpy mood since he woke up. What was going on here?

"Hey guys," she waved to the phone. "My husband and I are getting our first ride out of town." She giggled then amended. "The first rodeo with me fully awake, that is." She looked at Bill whose eyes had suspiciously narrowed on her.

"Let me scratch that, this is me and my fiancé. Geez, the air is so cold in here, after I called him my husband."

Bill snorted and turned to face the window as he viewed the landscape instead. Not flying the helicopter meant his attention could now take in the beauty of nature. God is good , he thought as he marveled at everything. Once they reached their destination, Innu gladly slipped her fingers into his and pulled him into the taxi which took them to a supermarket. She grabbed two huge trolleys, one for her and one for him.

"Will you stop giving me the eye and push," she commanded as she got into the shop and he trailed after her. He watched her animatedly talk to the woman at the veggie stall, the man at the butchery in the supermarket before she led him to the til.

"Am I not the luckiest girl on earth or what," she commented when the woman on the til continued to stare at broody Bill.

"Eye candy right." She winked and pushed her trolley away.

"Innu," Bill grumbled. When they got out, she let out a yelp, "Great she is here." She continued to push her trolley to an old beaten up Mazda bt50.

"Why are you standing there like a loony? Come on." Innu waved.

Bill rolled his eyes. He just was clueless over what was going on with her. He pushed the trolley with the heavy food stuff in it and some toiletries.

"It's nice to finally meet you Mr. Lewis," an old kindly looking woman greeted him.

"Bill please." He shook her hand and curiously looked at Innu. She winked and opened the back door for him after he stowed the last of the things at the back. "After you captain."

He was surprised when they drove downtown to the ghetto. The neighborhood in Prospectville reminded him of his old neighborhood in Harmony. They passed some dilapidated building which had people coming in and out from them. Children playing in the rugged road, who excused them before they passed then resumed with their game of soccer.

A few bars and construction sites were ahead until they stopped at a two storied building, full of graffiti drawings on the outside wall. The more he looked at the drawings, the more he realized that they were rather artistic and gave the place a certain air about them.

A couple of kids rushed to Innu to his surprise as she hugged them.

Innu, a question was in his eyes, as three women rushed to the back of the car to retrieve the goods.

"Welcome home Bill."

"Huh." He thought he hadn't heard her right. She sniggered. "Welcome home. Since I rejected Marg at her generous offer, this is where I stayed after my dad kicked me out."

"What?"

She giggled like his reaction was the funniest thing that she'd ever seen. She walked back to him and held his hand. "The inheritance honey, this is why I need it."

She kissed him on the chin, let him go and saucily walked away while he followed behind, stunned beyond words.

BILL MOANED AT THE melt in your mouth pork chops.

"It's good right," Jane Cooper, the old woman who had picked them up at the supermarket said.

"You bet." He took another bite. "Girl can cook."

He looked at Innu who was still serving the customers who had come into the restaurant. They were mostly men who appeared to be working on the construction site nearby. This also explained the plain tasty meal, stomach filling and scrumptious, not at all fancy like he had imagined when Marg spoke about Innu's catering days in high school then varsity. One of them said something to her and she giggled before she winked at him.

"Girl can cook and work tirelessly." Bill commented. He reached for the napkin and wiped his hands. Since they had gotten into the restaurant, Innu had been on her feet, preparing the dishes like a machine hotwired on the grid and barking out a few orders to the young ladies to get moving.

"You know, she once did a fundraiser for Sweetie." The old woman pointed to a girl dressed in a green tee shirt and black jeans. Sweetie looked like one, meant to be in highschool and definitely not working for a living.

"Sweetie got pregnant when she was fourteen and her parents threw her out. A single parent with nowhere to go, she turned to prostitution to survive. She'd rented a room here. I found her writhing in pain in her room when the labor pains started after seeing her last client. Innu happened to be passing by the door." Jane shook her head. "At that time Innu kept to herself. I called out to her for assistance. You should have seen how pale she got like a white sheet of paper when she saw the blood. Thank God she didn't pass out, because that was going to be mighty hard for me to deal with two people at the same time. She was of great help that night. Sweetie delivered a bouncing baby boy and I saw something in Innu too after the incident, hope. Her nana is an old friend of mine and she'd asked me to keep an eye on her. She was worried. Her eyes since I met her seemed dull, you know, like she'd lost something precious. She didn't eat much, and she wasn't taking good care of herself. It was like she'd lost the will to live. By seeing what Sweetie and the other girls were going through and how they fought despite the odds stacked against them, Innu got a new lease on life. She helped Sweetie after, with her little fundraising and pleaded with her to not return to that life. That's how she arranged for this room here to start her cooking business and employed Sweetie. That's Precious," Jane continued telling the stories of the girls who were helping Innu and apparently she had hired, to take care of the restaurant while she was away.

"I am growing old as you can see. This building was left by my late husband. It was part of the pension given by the government for his service. I thought of handing it over to Innu since I and my husband were never blessed with any children of our own. Innu has come to mean so much in the short time I have known her. Her grandmother is right, she is sweet to a fault and when she cares about people, it's all the way, no halves or quarters there."

Jane chuckled and Bill smiled at that.

"Innu refused for me to hand over the building to her like that, including when I sold it at a lower price. She made a couple of calls for the building to be valued and promised she would buy it from me. *What you need is a long vacation in the Bahamas,* she told me. While I informed her that if she failed to pay within a month, it would be sold to someone else. It was a joke on my part, yet to Innu it meant something else. The girl is stubborn and wants her way all the time."

Bill laughed at that thought. Yep, she truly was an amazing, tenacious and stubborn girl.

"Is this what you have always done?"

Jane shook her head. "The rooms were mostly rented out to students attending a nearby college. After my Tom passed, Precious approached me. She wasn't a student and didn't have anywhere to go. She worked three jobs waitressing and still the money wasn't enough for her to rent a decent apartment. So I decided to lease out a couple of rooms at a lower price. You know at times that the helping hand we offer goes a long way than you think."

Bill leaned in and smiled at her. She smiled back and swatted his arm. "I knew she found a charmer here. Stop looking at me like I am the only woman in your world." Bill laughed. He whispered something in her ear and her eyes widened.

"Serious."

"Yes," he nodded. She put out her hand and shook his before she pulled him and kissed him on the cheek.

"Well nice to finally meet you. Her dad was insistent, you know and I was debating over how to break the news to her. Should I tell her?" Bill shook his head and winked. "Let it be a surprise." Bill was enjoying the company of the old woman. He had seen Innu's plans after his little declaration to her father and the sale went through yesterday actually. He was quick to point out that it had to be Innu's choice that she wanted to get married to him, and not the fact that she had been put in her corner by the family.

Now seeing Innu acting like she was in love, he was having second thoughts if he should tell her here instead. What if she scrammed, his mind jokingly mocked.

Jane laughed and fumbled for something in her pocket.

"I think you deserve this." She motioned for him to stretch his hand and placed it in his palm.

Bill stared at it.

Forever, is what it was called and his mom had given it to him when he turned thirty. At that time, she had worked in the jeweler's shop for ten years. The Hastings had offered her a pick of their rings as a thank you for her ten years of service and of course to keep her with them, since she had turned out to be their best sales person.

"Put it on the woman that you love," she had said, when all he had wanted to do was protest and make her drop her expectations of him ever settling down.

"You recognize it. I gather you are the man who gave it to her."

Bill slowly nodded. "She was sad when she handed it to me as part of the down payment. She said she didn't know how she got it, but felt it had a significant meaning yet she couldn't remember anything."

"What is that," Innu happily asked and Bill slipped the ring into his pocket. "Mrs Cooper's little secret."

She frowned at him. "Are you done here? I have still got to show you something."

Bill pulled her hand and she landed on his lap. "Not until you eat something. You have been working non-stop." Another girl, June, if he was not mistaken, approached them with a basket in hand. "Right on time," Innu exclaimed.

"Don't worry. I will eat where we are going," she said and motioned to the basket. Innu stood up and Bill did the same.

He clasped at the old woman's hand and she hugged him.

"Be happy," she whispered in his ear. He smiled and followed Innu who appeared to be impatient to leave. Really was she going to cram more surprises on him in one day? He waved at the ladies who gladly waved back at him .

Innu took him to a place that overlooked a tiny harbor where they watched the sun setting. She was laying her head on his broad chest while his arms were wrapped around her. Tranquil is how the end of their day felt while Bill's hope rose that his woman was back to him again. The woman he had met three years back, so open and full of life. Ready to take on the world no matter what hurdles came her way.

"I used to come here the first months I started staying with Mrs. Cooper. I would sit here and watch the men go about their duties, simple lives yet they seemed content. I guess I drew my strength too from seeing them make a living. This is my happy place." She turned around to face him. "Did you ever have a happy place that you would go to?" Bill pointed to the sky and Innu frowned. He chuckled softly.

"A wise old man once said, if you are stuck and can't see ahead, go higher, you will be able to see the view from there."

She smiled. "I gather that was your gramps." He nodded.

He kissed the top of her head. "Don't you think we should be heading back to Harmony? Tomorrow is our big day. We will end up being the first couple to have missed our wedding."

She giggled and cradled his face in her hands.

"Bill Lewis. Did I ever tell you that you are a sweet guy," she asked and pasted a kiss on his cheek.

"And that even if it sounds crazy, I think you are hard to resist." She kissed him on the other cheek while he smiled at her playfulness.

"It's hard not to fall in love with you," she finished, then kissed him on the lips. Bill cradled her head, returning the kiss slowly before he pulled away and whispered. "It's hard not to fall in love with you too." Then they were kissing again, saying what their words couldn't fully put across. Innu softly moaned and pulled away. She took Bill's hand and slid it on her abdomen.

"Baby, public displays of affection in this manner will land us in prison. Is this punishment for yesterday?"

"Bill Lewis," She hissed softly and asked, "Can't you feel it."

"Feel what?"

She rolled her eyes at the hand that was now slowly stroking her and almost making her go nuts. She ground her teeth and held him still, before she traced the scar with his hand. "There," she said.

Bill inquiringly stared at her. Now that the time had come, she suddenly felt nervous and her mouth became dry. She shifted from their position on the blanket and stood up. Bill followed her.

"Love, what's wrong." He hugged her from behind.

She inhaled deeply then exhaled. Turned around to face him and answered in a low voice, "Three years ago, I went out to celebrate my birthday party with my family. We were booked at the Lakeside hotel. It has this appealing little club underground."

Bill smiled at the thought. Considering it was the very same club they had met. He was in a grumpy mood actually, after he had spotted Fletcher with his latest girl across the room.

He reached out to the phone on the ground, having dropped it in shock after seeing his dad in the club, when nicely red painted feet came and stood next to him. They were in peep toe, beaded heels that must have been impossible to walk in for someone else other than a model. He remembered running his eyes from her toes and up, thinking how can she have such long smooth legs exposed, is she even wearing anything. He was relieved when he saw the beginning of a metallic dress. The beautiful face took his breath away of course. He had known that such beautiful long legs belonged to a bombshell and he wasn't wrong.

"Like what you see," she had asked and Bill was won over further by her sultry voice, while his mind damned him for being such a weakling. Guess the fruit didn't fall further from the tree like he had thought. He was definitely a Fletcher. Beautiful things apparently made his mind zonk out

"Hi," he greeted and took a sip of his drink.

"I'm Innu by the way." She stretched her hand and he held it. She slightly gasped from his touch. Guess he wasn't the only one feeling that then, as they stood silently looking into each other's eyes like they had the whole day to be doing that. She cleared her throat.

"Oh, sorry. Bill Lewis." Then she had looked at him more closely, this time critically and not that hungry perusal she had been giving him and giggled.

"I will be damned. That's why I thought you seemed familiar. You are Margaret's infamous brother. You are a spitting image of Fletcher, I'm sure you must have heard that a thousand times."

Bill had grimaced, of course he had.

"I am Innocencia. Innu, crazy best friend." That's when it clicked to Bill on where he had heard her name from.

"Holy...,"he swore and she cut him off. "Hey don't swear." He laughed, a bit disquieted at the same time that this was Margaret's best friend. What were the chances of getting muddle headed over his little sister's friend?

"What are you doing here?"

She pointed to a table at the far end. "Celebrating with family." That's when she pointed to the tiara and sash which had the words *happy birthday princess* boldly written on it. It was official. He had stripped off her clothes to the point, he hadn't noticed the sash.

"Happy birthday is in order then," he said and she giggled. They shared a couple of shots afterwards as Bill winked at her and said it was in celebration of her being thirty two. Innu was game, and gladly gulped down the gin and maintained her cool composure throughout like she was drinking water.

Bill laughed at the fact that Marg was right. Her friend was crazy. They were outrageously flirting and the next Innu was dragging him to the dance floor and pulling out a dirty dancing routine on him that shot his blood to the roof, before she left him stunned on the dance floor after the words that her boyfriend would be announcing their relationship. The rest was history.

"I guess it must have been the shock of finding out that Dwayne was getting married to Mia that got to me the most because as it turned out I hooked up with four men that night and ended up pregnant. I couldn't remember anything while they were these men certainly not my type who were quick to say I had been with them. I was disgusted with myself. Had my life come to that? That I would sleep with low lives too. When I found out I was pregnant it got worse. I was having nightmares and I needed to get rid of the evidence on how low I had fallen, but I couldn't. I couldn't Bill and at the same time I hated this thing that was growing in me and loathed myself more."

The phone buzzed; interrupting them both while Bill tried to make sense of what Innu was talking about. Four men, huh.

It rang again, and he answered it without checking the caller id.

"What?" he yelled.

A few words were said and his jaw dropped.

"Bill," Innu touched his shoulder. He stared at her in confusion. "Innu can we continue this tomorrow. I need to go."

"Is something wrong?" she asked.

"I will explain," he turned around and started walking away. Innu felt deflated and at a loss. He must have thought of something because he turned around again, walked to her and gave her a delicious kiss that left her reeling and whispered. "Everything is going to be fine. Don't get yourself worked up. I love you and always will. Remember that," then he was gone.

CHAPTER 11

Norah was getting out of the house when her phone vibrated. She opened the message and yelped, then clamped her mouth with her hand. Boyd, her husband, looked at her.

"It's nothing love. Just go on ahead; I will join you at church." Boyd nodded and walked to the car while she retreated back into the house and punched the number.

"Elle what in the hell is that thing that you sent."

The agitated girl answered.

"What do you mean he has been with the child the whole night?" She yelled.

Elle was sobbing over how her husband's cousin had contacted Bill about the little accident.

"How could you be so careless after the money I have been giving you?"

"I am tired okay," She snapped. "You promised that he would come to me. It has been three years now and he still doesn't see me.

Norah briefly shut her eyes and ground her teeth. Dealing with amateurs was never a good idea.

"I am thinking of leaving. I need to start afresh, find a man who will love me and we have a family together."

"Wow, Elle and you think I will let you do that. Bill might be keeping you in the luxury that you longed for, but he is not paying your brother to keep his mouth shut. Imagine if that truth came out, that in a rage, you sent your brother and his men to attack my step daughter who happens to be his precious wife; it will not end well for you. Make sure you keep him there somehow and he doesn't leave anytime soon."

"How will I do that?" Elle protested.

"Figure it out. You are a clever woman," Norah yelledd. "I have a wedding to ruin. Just do your part," She finished with a huff, got out of the door and banged the door after her. She continued to make a call to Elle's brother, the man who hated Bill with all his might. He had one friend who was stuck on the wheel chair after that night, and two more who had left the life of crime, figuring they would meet someone else even worse than Bill who would kill them on the spot.

The sound of footsteps could be heard echoing in the house after she left. The man peeked through the drapes and watched her drive off. He sighed and pulled out his phone.

"Tate." He said. "It's time we had that talk that I've been avoiding."

BILL OPENED HIS EYES and sat upright on the chair, keeping watch of Reign who continued to sleep.

How could he have been so stupid, he thought, berating himself for the year he has been apart from him. If only he had taken that last step to see Reign like Tate had advised, then he would have known what he now realized has always been right beneath his nose.

He thought of how furious he was when Elle informed him that she was pregnant. Impossible since he still maintained that he wasn't with her that night. He wasn't fully aware of the game she was trying to play, hence kept her around because she was his friend, giving her the benefit of doubt until he overheard her telling those lies to her friends. She was proud of it too.

And to think he had forgiven her for spiking his drink!

"I got the stud, the black sheep in the Fletcher clan. He is mightily endowed and definitively attracted to women. Look at us now expecting our first child together."

Her girlfriends had asked to use his room so they held a little baby shower for her. Bill froze by the door, having come back to retrieve the locker keys he had forgotten before he hit the gym.

The beautiful, sweet girl, he still thought she was despite the lies she seemed to spew out of her mouth without compunction was lost there and then as the glossy tone she was using grated on him.

Elle must have sensed him by the door because she looked up and when the girl friends saw his stunned expression, they scrambled like a gun had sounded. Bill Lewis's anger was legendary when it did eventually blow up.

A week later Elle left. She resigned from her job without any notice to her friends' surprise and they never saw her again.

Ten months down the line, she reached out to him again. He would have blown the roof down, except she sounded weak and she was crying. Elle looked terrible when he first laid his eyes on her, with dark circles beneath her eyes while she clutched on to him for support and begged him to save their baby. She was staying at a small remote town, a place he could have never thought she would stay at. Reign was in the ICU, fighting for his life.

The sleepless nights soon followed as he made sure he kept watch of Elle and the baby. Just that one touch from the baby, his tiny hand clasped on his finger and Bill knew beyond a shadow of doubt. Reign was his. How much he had prayed then, thinking it was his fault why that little precious boy struggled for life. Reign did fight, despite the odds. Pneumonia had sent a lot of strong men down to an early grave yet here his son was, barely a month old and clutching for dear life.

A miracle is what it was, when he fully recovered. The tests were done and just like he knew, Reign was his. With that confirmation the doubts began.

Maybe Elle was right. He was with her. He was too drunk for his own good, so he had mixed up the details. At the same time he couldn't refute the truth that he was married to Innu. The ring said it. It was now split, meaning she had the other part.

He fought against his inadequacies at the realization that he had fathered a beautiful baby boy, defenseless in the world. Bill knew he would disappoint his son, just like his father had disappointed him over the years. He didn't want that, so he stayed away once Reign was in the clear.

Tate of course would insist he took an active role in his son's life. A fool is what he had been. Reign slowly opened his eyes and looked at him. Innu's voice filtered into his mind. *I got pregnant.*

"Hey little man," he greeted and Reign smiled at him. "Daddy," he said and scrambled from the bed into his arms.

Such a big boy, Bill thought and chuckled softly, hugging his little man. Guess Elle had always shown Reign pics of him for him to recognize him instantly. Or Reign was just so much like Innu, he easily trusted a person.

Norah's reaction made sense now. How she had seemed to quirk at his presence. She knew. Innu would never give up their son, even if she couldn't remember anything. He had seen her yesterday with those children at the restaurant, how they also adored her before she set about working.

Fletcher disliked him yes, but he knew deep down his father loved him in his own way. While Norah's look by the door when she saw them kissing was of deep loathing. It was the expression of a person who would do much more harm than good if given the chance.

The door opened and they both turned to it. Elle cautiously walked into the room and didn't look at him. Instead, she went to the bed and Reign gladly went into her arms. "Mummy." A look of wonder and love passed on her face.

Should he be relieved that she loved his son despite him not being hers?

"Where were you when Reign ate the peanuts?"

Elle licked her lips and continued to hold Reign. "I'd gone out on a few errands. Tate blew everything out of proportion. Look at the little guy. He is fine. It was just a mild reaction."

"Didn't you inform the maid that Reign was allergic to peanuts?"

She inhaled softly. "There's nothing in the house with peanuts in it. I didn't think there was a need to point that out to her. How was I to know that the girl scouts with their nutty chocolate bars would pass by the house and Reign would scream the roof down, forcing the maid to buy one for him?"

"Speaking of maids, what happened to Celeste?"

Ella shuffled her feet. She was nervous. The calm way in which Bill was addressing her signaled that the explosion will be a big one. She was shocked at seeing him in the ward after getting her coffee from the canteen. She should have known that Tate would call him. Damn Bridget's husband, always interfering everywhere.

The old maid was beginning to see too much. There's a time she pointed out to Elle that Reign looked like someone she knew. Then she said the name she always dreaded. Innocencia Lockwood.

She had to go away and fast. Considering this is the same small little town Innu stayed for the months she was expecting. Apparently Norah had won Innu's confidence at a time she was vulnerable and brought her here to give birth, so no one in their society realized that Innu was pregnant.

"Why did you do it," Bill asked her. She looked up at him. He was closely looking at her and she became more nervous. She didn't want to go to jail. Already her older sister was in there on embezzlement charges. She was no longer the sophisticated woman that she had admired and who had pulled strings for her so she worked as an airhostess, including getting the fake educational qualifications for her. When Bill offered to take care of her, she knew that would be the best deal for her. She wouldn't have to pretend to be something that she was not and having to look over her shoulder that one day, everyone would find out the truth. She still wanted this life more.

"Do what," she asked, feigning puzzlement.

"Separate mother and son?"

Elle shut her eyes. Her game was up. Her transgression had finally come to roost.

INNU WHIRLED AROUND and faced the door when she heard it being opened. She dejectedly slumped her shoulders and whined. "Oh it's you."

Her handsome step brother grinned. "Geez, do you have to be that obvious of the fact that I'm not him."

She giggled at his hurt expression and watched him widen his eyes in surprise. He rubbed at them. "I just didn't see that. You giggle at my dry sense of humor."

She snorted. This was the happiest day of her life after all, so she wasn't going to let his comments get to her in the least.

"What do you want Dwayne?"

His mouth turned downwards. "Guess I'm no longer the man of the hour in your life."

That mischievous streak came to the forefront. She stretched out her arms.

"Come on, hug time." She said, softly laughing at him. He pulled her into his arms and hugged her.

"Glad you found the love of your life and you are no longer pining after me—ouch." He stepped away after she stubbed his toe with her heeled shoes.

"That hurts," he whined.

"Good. Next time you will know when to open that trap of yours and spew out your nonsense."

Dwayne laughed and clasped her hands in his. "It's good to see you again, Innu." He said and sadly smiled. "I am sorry for what I put you through."

Innu shook her head. "Hey, this is my happiest day. No tears. And our history is water under the bridge."

They continued to stare at each other, smiling like they had done before their lives were turned upside down. A knock sounded and they guiltily looked at each other. Another knock had Dwayne scrambling for cover behind the rack of clothes.

"Really, why are you hiding there," Innu protested, while Dwayne shooed her away.

"What if it's Bill." She rolled her eyes.

"You didn't tell him we were involved once right. That man has this dominating possessive look when he looks at you. I wouldn't want to be on his bad side."

She giggled at the thought of Walt shaking in his shoes too. She called out, "come in," while Dwayne pulled the hangers in place.

Norah looked around the room. "I thought I heard voices." Innu pointed to her phone.

"It was just a well wisher. So...," she turned around to look at herself in the mirror. "What brings you here? Thought you would be out there acting like the mother of the bride." Innu of course was pulling her leg. She knew Norah wouldn't do that.

"There is nothing pretty about being left on the altar."

"Pardon." She sharply turned around to face her. "What are you talking about?"

Norah smirked. "Bill is not coming."

Innu shook her head. This time, her step mother was wrong and she wasn't going to let her win by believing in her hogwash. Bill loved her.

"He is coming. Do not worry. He might be late because he is attending to an emergency, but he will be here. He promised."

"Ooh, you mean just like your mom promised that she would come back before she rushed into the arms of a married man and died."

Innu sharply inhaled. "That's not what happened and you know it."

Norah narrowed her gaze and approached her. She handed her the phone. Bill was hugging a little boy in a room that looked like a hospital, his face soft and tender and full of love.

"That's his son. Guess he omitted to mention that he had one, and a wife."

"No," Innu shook her head in denial. "It can't be. Bill loves me, and besides his family would have been aware of this."

"Really, the black sheep of the family, who doesn't set roots. Whose father loathes with all his might. That's the man you trust."

"I'm sure there's a better explanation to this." Innu shifted further away from her.

She didn't want to listen to this. A sense of dread had already set in, traveling down her spine as she broke into a little sweat. No this was a joke. Norah was taunting her as she usually did. The phone she was still holding onto, winked at her with the new photo with the same clothes Bill had worn yesterday.

He did leave in a rush and never explained. This might have been the reason why.

"You can flip to the next pic if you want," Norah advised.

Innu briefly shut her eyes, opened them and scrolled, still not believing Norah. A beautiful woman holding a toddler, who definitely looked like Bill, looked straight at the camera with an assured air about her being a mother that Innu will never have.

Norah's face had a triumphant smirk on it. "He's been married for five years. Imagine that. And his family is completely clueless. Who knows, maybe he has other women in each city. Like father, like son."

"Why." Innu asked her then turned to face her. "Why do you hold so much animosity against me when I've never tried to hurt you in any way? All these years I've stayed as far away from you as I could. Now here you are, spewing lies in my face about Bill."

Norah looked at her in disbelief. "You're still deluded huh. I've just exposed your knight and you think I'm against you. Innu can't you see you're the one at fault here love. Just like your mother, you take men that were never yours in the first place. What do you expect at the end? That they will leave their happy homes to settle with you, is that it?"

Innu clutched at her throat and shook her head in denial.

"No."

Bill would have told her if he had a family. Then her mind stopped to function as a thought suddenly settled in. The ring. How could she discount that as something fashionable that Bill had always worn? He had two rings that he used to wear. One was on his index and the other on his ring finger.

An anguished sob was released from her lips.

Norah laughed. "Now you realize the truth, don't you darling."

A shuffle of movement from the clothing rack had Norah looking at it before she smirked at an already distraught Innu then she walked out of the room.

Dwayne swore as he came out from behind the clothes and clutched at Innu's shoulder. "Little sis, don't let her words get to you. This is enough." He stormed out of the room.

Innu still clutched at her chest as tears slid down her throat.

Betrayed, again. Why? Why did they always do this to her? Whenever she thought, she could finally be happy; her castle would fade away in an instant as she discovered the lies beneath.

She desperately held onto the dressing table before she gave in to the darkness this time instead of trying to fight it.

The sound of the door almost being wretched from the hinges before it got shut with a bang had Norah turning around to see a furious Dwayne.

"Why are you coming out of there?"

Dwayne grabbed her hand and flung another door open before he pulled her into the room and shut the door behind them. "What were you looking for in that room," she yelled.

He glared at her. "Why did you do that? How can you be so vindictive?"

"Dwayne! Do not raise your voice to me. I am your mother."

He snorted. "No you are not. My mother wouldn't have been so vindictive of a person like Innu who will never hurt a fly."

"Innocent. Do you hear yourself? Innocent. She has pulled wool over your eyes. Is that it? Like mother, like daughter. Didn't you see the train wreck that she was from the word go. Prancing around with all those men. Parading them like her mother."

"Mother!" Dwayne yelled.

"Isn't that the truth? Of all people, imagine how betrayed I felt by my own son when you fell for her."

Dwayne wanted to deny it but he couldn't because she was right. He fell for Innu hard and instead of panicking the first time they kissed since for starters she was his step sister, he was thinking I want to date and marry her in a few months. And that is what he did, dated her without their parents being aware. She was fun, outgoing, sweet and a darling, very surprisingly naïve to some things and their sex was off the charts. He knew his mom and the general didn't have that sort of normal marriage, hence it didn't seem like a taboo to him to be taking a bite at the cookie.

On the night of her birthday, he and Innu had decided to disclose their relationship to the parents, except he found himself announcing his engagement to Mia instead.

An ultimatum is what the general gave him before he told him about his relationship with Innu.

"It was you who told the general about Mia and her pregnancy."

His mother chuckled softly. "I'm so sorry for ruining your little plan. Besides, you did sleep with Mia. That son was on you and not me."

Yes indeed, a mistake he made five months before he even dated Innu. He was reeling from shock that night when the general told him to do right by Mia. He hadn't been aware that she was pregnant for goodness sake.

How he had felt helpless then as he looked to the woman he loved and announced that he was marrying another. The hurt he saw in her eyes is what got to him more. He took what was meant to be the happiest day of her life and turned it into the worst by just the flick of his finger, and that guilt has consumed him ever since.

He tried to call her after she walked away from the table. Mia was clinging on his side like a second skin, not having expected that from him. How in the hell hadn't he noticed she was pregnant. She looked fuller in her body size. When he asked her once they were in the room, that's when she confessed to having hidden it from everyone and how she tied a corset around her middle to hide it.

He never questioned how the general found out, more concerned with where Innu had disappeared to, hence left Mia in the room in search of his love.

Innu answered his call, eventually to his relief, and assured him that she was okay. He wasn't convinced. He had to see her and she wasn't forthcoming about where she was, so he drove through town, to the spots they had frequented together until he saw her walking in a daze and on the verge of walking right into moving traffic. He ran to her before that happened. She was trembling, tears falling from her eyes before she slumped into his arms in a faint.

"Mom, what did you do to Innu?" He asked and looked at her with a hint of malice in his eyes.

"What I should have done to keep your father from being with her mother."

He looked at her in disappointment. "Dad was right in wanting to leave you. You are crazy." Was all he said before he rushed out of the room.

The general was opening the door to the dressing room.

"Bill still not here," He said in his gruff voice and for the first time, the good humor that always showed on his features was gone.

Dwayne nodded and they got into the room. Innu lay on the floor. Not breathing. Dwayne rushed past the general calling her name before he knelt down and checked her pulse.

CHAPTER 12

Three years ago.

"This must hurt." Innu gasped at the bruise on Bill's body and ran her hand, cringing to the thought that she was probably hurting him by pressing the part that was slowly turning purple. It ran across his shoulder, the bat having been applied with the full pressure that would have broken the bone. She thought over how he'd skillfully avoided getting the full brunt of it before he punched the face of one of the perverts who had been after her.

The sound of crushing bone had been heard from that blow, including the scream of terror from the perv before he lunged at two more of the men who still had some fight in them. Her heart had gone up to her throat when one of them waved a pocket knife at him.

"Are you superman or what," she asked in awe and reached out to the first aid kit. She quickly put a bandage on his side since he still bled there.

"I wish," Bill snorted. He removed the bandage and motioned for a mirror.

"This has to be stitched up."

She was trembling from the adrenaline rush and looked at him like he was nuts.

"No, no. We need the hospital and fast."

Bill reached for another bandage, and then he caught hold of her hand. "Sweetie, I know you can do this. I don't like hospitals and another thing; a police report will need to be filed over why I am like this. I hate the long process since I need to fly out tomorrow." He wasn't in any condition to fly out to anyway; she thought and clamped her mouth closed. She knew if she was to point that out, they would start arguing again and they had been doing much of that since he rescued her from that gang. His stubbornness and hers had made them remain at a stalemate.

She looked around the room and reached out for the whiskey then took a gulp, and winced. What was the use of letting him bleed out to death? It was an exaggeration on her part of course. Bill had seen that he needed only a few stitches and she had ascertained the same.

She handed the bottle to him and they set up the things. Sterilizing the instruments first. She would sew his skin up like a rag doll. She could do this. Her basic nursing course had taught her this after all.

She took in another swig and Bill laughed.

"This is crazy, you know, and so far, I have been doing the craziest of stuff today. Now I am stitching you up, half drunk and all because for some reason you think I can do it."

Bill laughed again. He took a swig of the alcohol and poured some of it on the wound.

"Don't worry love, I'm used to this."

"I don't know if that's meant to comfort me or what. Knowing that Margaret's brother has been stitched up a lot of times. Help me Lord," she whimpered, and then set about with her work. After she bandaged the stitches, she attended to the minor cuts on his forehead from the knife that he managed to tackle from the perv and he flinched. For such a man who had taken it all, really.

"Such a baby," she muttered, then reached for the swabs. Bill laughed and his handsome face had Innu's heart flattering to a different beat from the one she had felt earlier. "It hurts."

"Ha, ha, very funny Bill. You should have thought of that before you took on four men at one go. You could have been killed."

Bill flinched again and narrowed his eyes on her. "Is that the thank you I get for helping out a damsel in distress? You are a piece of work you know. I was saving you from the lot and you stopped me by ordering me to let them go. It was enough, they have learnt their lesson. Do you think they would have let you go?"

She stuck out her tongue. He laughed, the deep throated chuckle doing more to her giddy nerves, her attraction for him coming to the forefront. It was funny that Dwayne had even dared her.

She had disbelievingly looked at him when he suggested she hook up with anyone in the club. If she was serious about them, she wouldn't fall for a guy in an instant and he would disclose their relationship to their parents.

Dwayne was being a chicken, and she had known that, yet she humored him. That's when she spotted Bill at the bar counter. How could she not, with his impressive height and broad shoulders. A lady was on his side, animatedly chatting with him before she excused herself, and Innu took the opportunity to approach him.

When his phone fell and she stood next to it, his perusal of her legs, the appreciation, blew her away.

The first eye contact and she was a goner. She had been hit by a sledgehammer, not having thought it would happen to her in that manner. She was so confident that she would never fall this hard. Dwayne was it and as it turned out, she was wrong.

"You remind me of my little sis. What were you doing out there by the way?"

"Breathing in the fresh air," she simply answered. She didn't want to think about her hurt pride when Dwayne made the announcement of him and Mia to the family. Then Norah confronted her. Norah has always known about her and Dwayne. This was one huge mess. She forced her mind to concentrate on the task at hand, making Bill comfortable.

"Good for you too, Marg is my friend, so you can actually handle my naughtiness."

Bill frowned and advised. "Try to do your breathing exercises in a safe hood next time. If I hadn't followed you, you would be in trouble now."

Innu slowly nodded. "By the way, what happened to the bimbo who was all over you?"

"Elle." Bill grimaced and flinched when she dabbed more of the betadine on a cut on his cheek.

"Yes, her. I can't believe she almost scratched my eyeballs for taking your drink."

Bill rolled his eyes. "She's a drama queen. I sent her off to bed."

Innu giggled. "Did you give her pelvis a massage while at it?"

Bill's eyes widened on that note and she giggled further. He really could pull off the outraged expression. She continued with the task at hand while she mulled over her crazy birthday.

"Wanna talk about it." He was curiously staring at her. That's when she realized she had stopped attending to his cuts. She scrambled from the bed and walked away. A slight shiver passed down her spine, from the loss of warmth she was experiencing while she had been next to him.

"Are you sure you do not need the hospital?" Innu asked as she threw out the used cotton swabs into the tiny bin in the room and peeled off the gloves.

She could sense it, that he moved from the bed and came to stand close to her. This was crazy. One moment she had been hurt over Dwayne's betrayal and the next, here she was, fighting the urge not to fling herself on her best friend's brother. The feelings she had fought while they were in the bar before she had dragged him to the dance floor and plastered her body on his like a second skin, coming to the surface.

She knew what she was doing to him, feeling his breath tease her neck, the hard chest beneath her palms. How his heart had beat at a fast rate while they slowly moved to the beat of the music, the movements seductive and a slow tease to the both of them like they were literally mating on the dance floor. In that crowded room full of people, with the loud music and the flickering lights, they only had their eyes on each other.

People were indeed right about her. She was an unfaithful woman and she would forever remain that. She wrapped her arms over her chest. Bill touched her shoulders and turned her around.

"Please don't look at me in that way."

"What way," he asked and narrowed his eyes.

"Like you care."

"What makes you think I don't care?"

She nervously giggled. "The fact that I finally met Margaret's infamous crazy brother."

He frowned and looked around. "I'm waiting for the drum roll, since for some reason, that is supposed to mean something right, which I'm failing to get?"

She snorted then shifted away. "Apart from the fact that vulnerable Innu usually latches on to the next handsome man, who thinks he is too smart for his good, when she is at her lowest point."

Bill threw back his head and laughed. "Do you fear that you might do that because of the way that I am looking at you?"

She stamped her feet in exasperation. He wasn't taking her seriously like all the men who always managed to come in her sight. She was vulnerable and she knew that if she didn't get out of the room, she would do something that she would regret for life. Yes he had come to her rescue when she least expected it. When her body had been stunned to the point she had stood in a stupor, unable to fend off those lecherous men who had attacked her, his voice was the one that had stopped them in their tracks. "I wouldn't do that if I were you," he had said.

"Why not," one of the men who appeared to be the leader had asked with a sneer on his face.

"Because that is my woman that you are planning to grope, and I do not share. Tell you what; if you can beat me, maybe you will have a go at it." The leader sneered while Innu gasped in outrage.

"Wait." Bill said, stopping them with his hand, "what the heck. Just come at me, all four of you," he said then smiled that quirky smirk she had come to like before he removed his jacket and rolled his sleeves.

The self assurance, the disregard over their weapons they had in hand, a baseball bat, a bottle and the fact that they were four and he one, made them laugh with glee at how stupid he was. Except as it had turned out, they were wrong and were probably in hospital now, nursing their wounds.

"We are both alike. You and I," Innu whispered. A brow furrowed on his face and she resisted the urge to smother it down with a kiss.

"We are wanderers who will never set up roots. Which for some reason I was contemplating for a couple of months now except ..."she choked, not believing that she was about to cry again and make a fool of herself.

"As usual, I have been put in my place."

That one touch from him, as he grabbed her hand and engulfed her in a warm hug took the strength away from her and she wept. Giving in to the despair, heartache, frustration and pain she has always suppressed with her sunny smiles. Her step mother's voice drifted through in her mind, *you will never be good enough for any man. Your use darling is for sex only. When a man wants to settle down, they will never choose you.*

She sobbed harder, clutching on his strong arms as he soothed her, feeling guilty at the same time and full of despair. How could she cry like this and at the same time want this man who soothed and comforted her in this manner.

"Harsh baby, everything is going to be alright."

For a second she let herself believe that Bill meant what he was saying. That what had hit her in those few moments when their eyes met, had hit him too. His deep voice was so sure that her life wasn't bleak in the way she perceived it.

Holding her tightly and running his hand on her back in comfort, wasn't the incorrigible flirt her best friend had spoken about, but a man who truly cared if she was hurting.

"Hey." He said and pulled away slightly. Cupped her face in his huge hands and looked deeply into her eyes.

"Hey, let's wipe those tears off sweet cakes. No use looking like a panda."

She snorted. She became aware too of the fact that he hadn't put back his shirt on. His skin was silk and hard beneath her hands that were wrapped around him. She ran her hand on his back, her fingers slowly gliding down before they came to the bandage on the side

"Does it still hurt?"

"Just an irritable ache," he answered, his voice sounding tight for some reason. She looked up at him, the eyes told her everything. He was aroused beyond measure by their closeness. That's when she became aware of his body's response to her, and she had thought she had it bad for him.

"Kiss me," she simply said.

"Innu, you are vulnerable love," he whispered. She shook her head, cupped his face and kissed him.

Bill nearly protested from that one single kiss except his body hummed in response and he found himself cradling her head and deepening the kiss. She tasted so sweet like honey, the way he had imagined she would taste when they danced together on the dance floor and she had leaned in to naughtily whisper those damned words that had him reeling in shock and almost sweeping her off her feet so he took her to his room and made her come to her senses.

Bill groaned and ran his hand down her back, stroking and knowing full well that she will never forget his touch, no matter how she will try to do so.

He opened the zip to her dress and ran his hand on her back massaging the places where he knew she probably wasn't aware to be sensitive.

Her breathing heightened and she drew deeply into the embrace. He cupped her bottom, easily picked her up from the ground and wound her long legs around his waist before he walked to the bed with her.

"Bill please," she implored, suggestively moving those hips and reaching for the belt, desperate for him like he was for her. He knew he wouldn't last. This was going to be fast, but next he would take her slow.

They panted, kissed and touched.

He slid his hand into the back pocket to reach out for his wallet and opened it, while he pressed butterfly-like kisses on her face and swore as he came to nothing apart from his credit cards and 100 dollar notes.

Innu pulled back and stared at him, her eyes bright and full of desire and her breath coming out in short little pants.

"Please, please don't tell me you do not have protection on you," she said, despair tingeing her voice.

He briefly shut his eyes and nearly mumbled, *damn it Henderson*.

He opened them and nodded. "Let's just say three months ago I discarded all my protection when I decided to stop having sex."

She incredulously looked at him before she giggled.

"Laugh all you can love."

She was still laughing when she asked. "How is that working for you?"

"Honey, I'm about to expire on the spot. I nearly took you on the dance floor."

Innu squirmed and reached out to him. He held her hand and shook his head. She got it. He would definitely expire. She lightly bit on her bottom lip. She has never had sex without protection. She was always careful about these things, afraid of bringing a child into her confused life.

"Three months huh," she asked.

"Yes. I did the tests too and the whole work. This man here is clean."

Innu giggled at that. "I am not going to ask how many sexual partners you have been with cause hey, you are a Fletcher after all."

Bill cradled her head and kissed her deeply before he pulled away. "Are you not on birth control?" She shook her head. "It messes up my system, so latex is what I prefer."

Bill thought of his vow to never put a woman in the family way and slightly shifted.

"By the way, don't be too quick to judge that I am a Fletcher. In truth my sexual partners do not even reach these five fingers."

She was shocked when he said that, and then he winked at her, she knew he was probably joking. He couldn't be serious.

"What about you, when was the last time?"

"Last time was with my boyfriend, a week ago. We did the tests together too, so both of us were clean and I still insisted on protection."

"I gather the boyfriend is the same one you were raving about on the dance floor." She nodded and shifted away. Since she wasn't the type to have raw sex, she saw that it was useless to continue in the position they were in.

Bill shifted again to give her the space to move. She tugged on her zip and she froze when he reached out to pull it up and he too dragged his pair of trousers and belted them in place, though it did nothing to hide his arousal.

He sat next to her on the bed and took that bottle, seeing there was no way of stopping his desire for her that still coursed down his veins, apart from drowning it out with the spirits.

"I can still help you out with your discomfort," she offered and got a roll of the eyes in answer.

"What happened?" Bill asked her instead.

Innu took a swig when he handed her the bottle. She drew her knees and wrapped her arms on them after she took a swig and handed it to him. Bill caught sight of the beautiful feet.

"Cute," he motioned to the little toes.

She snorted. "Well. I hate them. An engagement is what happened."

Bill frowned at her and she guessed he most probably thought she was now cheating the so-called fiancé with him.

She waved her ring less fingers. "To his secretary and that secretary is not me, but Mia."

"Oh Innu." Bill cradled her face and looked at her with compassion in his eyes. The tears started anew. She dashed them off with the back of her hand. "It's no big deal Bill. It's not like it's the first time a guy has bailed out on me. I mean I'm the worst and can't stay faithful to one man. He is better off with someone else. Mia is sweet and charming."

Bill growled and held her shoulders before he shook her. "Don't do this to yourself. You deserve a good man who will love you and not make you feel less about yourself. How many men have bailed out on you?"

"Bill, just forget it." She moved away from him, got up from the bed and walked to the door.

"Innu, how many men have bailed out on you," he demanded and shifted to where she now stood, turned her around to face him and gave her the probing look on her face.

"Too many to count." She finally admitted. "I keep on going back on the saddle thinking, maybe he was never the one for me. I will surely find, '*the on*e."

Bill gazed at her in wonder. "Marg said you're the one who always bails out when things begin to get serious."

She chuckled mirthlessly. "Marg isn't aware. Every time when I tell her I bailed, it's because I will be too ashamed to admit that I gave my heart to someone and it got stomped on again like it was nothing. Worldwise Innu, who always has men lining up for her, is just a pathetic little girl who can't seem to make the right choice where men are concerned and always ends up with the player. Classic right. The only thing I'm good for is sex but when it comes to marriage, oh honey you are too out there. Your mother's pic was once splashed on the tabloids with her lover. Like mother like daughter."

Bill sharply inhaled over that and held on tight to her shoulders. "I only bailed out on one guy in my life," she continued.

Bill wiped the tears that seemed to be so close by. The hurt and pain in her eyes reminded him so much of himself. Hadn't he loathed it too when everyone was quick to point out his father's misdeeds to him. Worse off, he was the spitting image of Aaron Fletcher, so he was definitely like him. All were assumptions that people made without getting to know him.

"Walter was his name. He was so sweet and kind and thought I discredited myself all the time. We were happy, you know. Until he started being paranoid. The novelty of our love wore off quicker than a wax candle. One moment, we were so in love and the next he started keeping tabs on me. Where I had been, with whom I had been with oh not to forget the one question that was now always at the tip of his tongue, did I sleep with the guy." She chuckled softly on that note and continued.

"It didn't help matters that Walt had said we should wait where intimacy was concerned, so how could I prove to him that he was the only one I wanted. One night, on one of my catering gigs, at a reunion, my waitresses left me to pick up everything on my own. They disappeared, including your little sister. Bloody Henderson had taken her."

Bill laughed at the glare she produced when she spoke of Garret. "Since it was my business, I couldn't bail out like the rest of them. I had to make sure that all my things were packed up, take the inventory

over what had been broken and drive back to school. It was around
five in the morning when I got there. Walt was already pacing in front
of my room, eyes red from lack of sleep and I guess he had drunk a
bit too. The first thing that came out of his mouth was, how many
were there. Imagine that. I was tired from all the running around I had
done the whole evening and the picking up afterwards and here was an
insecure young man demanding to know how many men I had given
my precious cookie to. How I wished to have participated in an orgy
that had broken out after the party. It sounded much more appealing
than the accusations that I was facing while I fought down the fatigue."

Bill wiped the tears that still fell from her eyes. Innu sniffled. "From
then on, our relationship went south. It hurt to be so in love and yet
to have this person who said he loved me but did not trust me. I did
try to get back at Walt by the way, by cheating on him. My one night
stand turned into a night vigil since your little sister by that time had
her differences with Garret and when she saw me with the man, she
decided to hold a night vigil outside my door. Praying as loud as she
could, including banging the door like a drum."

Bill pulled Innu into his arms. How she seemed so lost and
vulnerable. Nothing at all like the seductress everyone who knew her,
described her as.

"Finally I ran off with Drew to Italy. Not in the sense of course
that everyone thinks. But you know people; apparently they are always
quick to conclude the worst where I am concerned.Drew had huge
dreams of joining the fashion world and I thought why not. Daddy
gave me a few bucks to spare. I became his business partner. We opened
up a clothing retail outlet in Milan. Then six months down the line
when I thought things were going so well and, yes we had started
messing around together, I found a note on the door. He had upped
and left the city. Sold everything like it was his to begin with, all
because at that time my daddy had decided enough was enough. He
was no longer sponsoring my little dream, in this case his. Apparently

Drew had made a few errors in our business and owed people money. Since my daddy had stopped the little well, he knew he was in hot soup, didn't give me a heads up and I was left to deal with the repercussions. The gullible Innu had fallen in love with a bastard out for her money yet again and who wrung her out to dry out with a bunch of goons when trouble licked on his heels. And do you know the story that was spewed out. Innu has done it again with her one night stands. Who of course will believe a serial cheater like me? I am my mother's daughter. I admit I have had my share of one night stands but when I am in a relationship I do not cheat. It's the other way."

"Oh Innu," Bill growled at that.

"So you see," she bravely smiled. "My skin is made of the thickest hide and my heart is stone. This is no big deal."

Bill shook his head in denial. "Sweetie it is a big deal, which I need to rectify."

"What are you doing?" She yelped when he picked her up from the ground and slightly winced from the ache on the shoulder and on the side. She hadn't realized he had now put on a clean shirt.

"Woman, we are getting hitched, then of course we pass by the drug store to get the protection, come back here and we have mind-blowing, body numbing sex, if you up to it, you can offer that relief then and I will definitely chow the cookie to the point, you will realize you've been hanging around assholes."

"You are out of your mind." A passionate kiss that muddled up her mind was placed on her lips as she wound her arms on his neck.

"Now you realize it. What had you called me? The infamous crazy Fletcher, not that I appreciate that title." She giggled. "Why not, I think it's intriguing, it lets you enjoy the benefits of sounding all elusive and mysterious."

Bill snorted.

"I'm serious. It's better than Cliff the loan shark, Godfrey the womanizer, Leo the bulldozer, Denzel the bully."

"My brother is not a bully," Bill protested.

"Yah, tell that to the woman he bullied to marry him."

"Marg told you that." She giggled.

"Keep at it and I will drop you." She yelped and clutched harder on his neck, safe in his strong arms as she sniffed on his neck and thought she would never grow tired of how glorious he smelt."

"Bill."

"Yes love."

"A little bit of warning, I can be vindictive when lied to."

"Cool, I am the same."

Innu giggled on that note. Marg did mention that about Bill's vindictive nature too. Like he could toss a bombshell, the way he did with his damning words to Garret, then apologized later to Marg, stating that he knew Garret loved her.

"I did date a couple of guys to piss my old man off. I really did like those guys. Their friendship meant more and when it came to sex, well it left me feeling empty. I felt like a fraud."

"Wait what."

Bill silenced her with another kiss and muttered softly that she thought she had imagined it. "When I fall, it's hard too, like right now. I know that I Love you as crazy as it sounds."

She stared at him in surprise and he had the audacity to wink like he hadn't said anything. She snorted as he walked down the flight of steps with her in his arms like she weighed nothing.

"Hey Bill. Can this be on a temporary basis?"

"Why," he asked with a frown.

"In case you too decide that you are tired of me."

Bill shook his head and rolled his eyes. "Never darling. I will never tire of you, besides Marg forgot to tell you this. I commit."

CHAPTER 13

Innu abruptly opened her eyes and screamed. A hand grabbed her and engulfed her in a hug.

"Honey, it's going to be okay." Her father soothingly said.

"Something is wrong. Bill should be here," she yelled and tried to scramble from the bed. Dwayne came into the room and looked at her pityingly.

She clutched at her heart. "Why are you looking at me like I am mad? Bill wouldn't hurt me. Dad, Dwayne." She imploringly looked at them."I am sorry Innu."

"No," she shook head vehemently.

"A connection, that's what we had from the start and we still have that even though right now it's faint, like something is wrong."

She tried to evade Dwayne who barred her path in the ward. Her father sadly looked at her like she was having a mental breakdown. The same expression she had seen on Dwayne's face. Norah got into the room.

"Where is he?" Innu yelled.

Norah looked at her in confusion, "What are you talking about?"

Innu glared at her. "You know damn well what I am talking about, where is my baby Norah. I can still hear his feeble cries."

"Norah what is Innu talking about," her father asked. A nurse got in after Norah with two orderlies.

"Darling, it must be the mental breakdown again. Remember you told me her mother used to have those. She is just confused."

Innu ran to her father and clasped at his arm, tears running down her face. "Daddy, believe me. Norah is lying. I remember the voices. I was in so much pain and it was raining that day. The baby was late in coming so they ended up inducing the birth. The excruciating pain, the confusion and everything else going on at the same time, I was sweating heavily and I couldn't move or breathe. I remember one of the people in attendance saying I needed a hospital quickly and she refused. She refused. I could have died there in that godforsaken place and no one would have known because she had convinced me that no one was meant to know about my condition. You would be disappointed if you found out that your princess had fallen pregnant and didn't know who the father of that child was. While everyone would be quick to mock me, that I had screwed up again. It was expected after all."

"Boyd she is out of it." Norah said sharply. "You can't be listening to these ramblings darling. How could I have been in Sweet valley and Prospectville at the same time?"

The orderlies were drawing close. "Norah. How do you know Innu was in Sweet valley when she didn't mention the place's name?"

Norah widened her eyes and shrugged. "Wild guess, and besides I have always sent your men to keep an eye on her. Whatever bothered you bothered me too and Innu has always been in your heart."

"Please daddy believe me." Innu begged. "Don't send me to the psych ward. I am not like mom." That seemed to snap Boyd out of the despair written on his face when she said that. He held up his hand.

"Boyd, what are you doing? You can't believe what she is saying," Norah stridently said.

The door to the ward opened again. "I believe her," Jeremy said and got into the ward.

"You," his mother shrieked at him.

He was holding a boy who looked like he was four or five years old in his arms. The beautiful woman that Innu had seen in the pic followed behind, and a couple of policemen.

"What is going on?" Boyd asked.

"Make sure you retrieve her phone. It will reveal a couple of leads for you."

"What is going on?" Norah's voice had turned into panic.

"Norah Lockwood you're under arrest for the kidnapping of Reign Lewis..."the policeman continued to recite her crimes. "And last for the attempted murder of Bill Lewis. You have the right to remain silent..."

Everyone in the room gasped in shock and Innu fainted.

FAST FEET ECHOED DOWN the hospital corridor before they broke into a full run. Innu's long wedding gown couldn't hamper her from running to the emergency room. After they revived her, Jeremy informed everyone of what he partly knew about what his mother did to Innu and how she lied to her on what happened the night of her party. Since Innu couldn't remember anything that happened that day, the whole day removed from her mind, Norah and Dwayne had been the ones to fill up the missing pieces.

Dwayne's confession over the fact that he was getting married to Mia partly worked to Norah's advantage on the decisions that Innu might have made that day.

Elle was crying as she handed Reign to Innu, while Reign cried too, even though not understanding what was happening. The rest of the family members had rushed to support the Fletchers while Norah and Elle were taken into custody. Innu was left stunned in the room, still not believing what she had been told. Her father, even though shocked by the news, had taken it in his stride and was playing with the weepy child. They all held their breaths when Reign smiled, that mischievous twinkle that would appear in both Innu and Bill coming to the forefront. The child had taken after both of them.

She found the family waiting outside the ER.

"Innu," Marg rushed to her. "Are you okay?" Innu nodded.

"The light truck came out of nowhere. He was crossing the street to the church, rushing to get to you."

Innu could imagine the horror that those who had witnessed the accident must have gone through.

Bill's mom came to her and they hugged. They stood for quite some time, comforting each other while Fletcher bellowed to Leo and Godfrey. "Please do something, don't just stand there. Save your brother."

"Dad, relax. He is in expert hands," Leo said but Fletcher continued hollering until they removed him from there.

Claudine reached out for something in her handbag and handed it to Innu. It was Bill's wallet and the black velvet box. "These were on him." She said, Innu nodded.

Claudine hugged her and walked away. Innu looked at the box that seemed slightly familiar to her. She slowly opened it and gasped. A beautiful ring was nestled in it. Not just any ring, but the one she handed to Jane as a down payment for the building. Along with what had been left of her money after the general threw her out of the house.

She noticed that another ring was seamlessly attached to it, to complete it. Bill's ring that he always wore and everyone seemed to not question over the significance. Maybe because he would have masked it by the other ring on his index finger and everyone thought he was just being fashionable Bill.

Her mind seemed to partly unravel when she ran her finger on the ring. Bill separating the ring, she was still dressed in her birthday outfit while he too looked at his worst with the cuts on his face. The happiness that shined through his eyes deflected her from seeing anything else. Pastor Jones was sniggering on the side and remarking. *I guess that's why I delayed leaving town. I had a feeling another crazy couple would need my help before the day ended.*

Bill winked at Innu. "Can't believe you are now a married woman right."

"I can," she retorted. "Since I am so in love with my husband. It was love at first sight where I am concerned."

Bill inhaled sharply.

"What, don't look at me like I have sprouted a few horns on my head. I admit Bill, from the first moment I saw you in the bar, I had to approach you."

"I am sorry to disappoint, but I don't believe in love at first sight," Bill airily said and she huffed and pinched him. Now he was pretending that he hadn't said the words first.

"Lust at first sight is what it is." He walked ahead while she chased after him, yelling at him to stop being absurd because he felt it too and Minister Jones was laughing at their antics. When they got out of the door, he swept her off her feet, she yelped and he gave her a passionate kiss before he whispered. "I love you too sweetheart," then went on to spell out what they would do for the remainder of their night.

Innu's tears flowed once again as everything hit her hard like a wave and she was left reeling from the impact. Bill was her husband!

He has always been hers from the moment they met and now she might lose him for good. She let out a sob and Marg who was silently on by her side, hugged her.

BILL STIRRED AND INNU abruptly raised her head. She had fallen asleep, still clutching at his hand. It was a week after the accident. Reign lay on the couch in the ward, with a crayon in hand and a coloring book in front of him. They sure had given birth to a quiet child who would one day be the next Picasso with the way he loved colorings away, including on the walls to Harriet's chagrin and her nana's delight.

"Baby." She stared at him as he slowly opened his eyes.

"Hey," he greeted, his voice scratchy from the lack of use.

"You gave us a scare there," she whispered and pressed the little button on the side of the bed to adjust it.

"Comfortable," she asked, fluffing the pillows a bit. He nodded. She took the glass of water on the side and placed a straw into it before she helped him drink. Reign must have heard them talking because he turned his head to them then scrambled from his position, walked to the bed and climbed on it.

"Daddy," he cried. He lunged at him with all the might of a Fletcher, having inherited his father's strong physique. It was debatable that he was even two years old.

"Hi little man," Bill greeted with a wince. His ribs ached like hell. Reign smiled up at him and Bill shut his eyes briefly.

"I am sorry Innu," he said gruffly. She grabbed his hand. "Why should you be sorry? You did nothing wrong."

He shook his head. "I didn't try harder to find you and clear the misunderstanding when I woke up with Elle in bed and not you. One minute I shut my eyes to your beautiful face and the next I open them and find her next to me. To top it all when I finally saw Reign, I should have thought of asking them to do a test on her too. I never once thought that she would do that. Take someone's child and pass him as hers. If only I had insisted on seeing Reign and this would have been cleared long back. His smile would have told me everything I needed to know, that he has always been yours."

"No Bill, don't blame yourself for my step mothers actions and Elle's. You hear me." She squeezed his hand in comfort. Before he could say anything, the door burst open and his whole family got into the room in a rush while the doctor tried to make them calm down. After he was done examining Bill, he left them with an order that they don't strain him.

Marg stood by the door while Fletcher appeared to be slightly pained at being on the outskirts instead of enjoying Bill's company like everyone else.

Bill stretched out his hand towards him and Marg wheeled him into the ward. Everyone was silent and a pin would have fallen and been heard.

Once they reached Bill's bed, Fletcher clasped his hand and gruffly said. "I am sorry son for everything."

Bill smiled. "Thank you for everything."

"Pardon," Fletcher looked behind him then back at Bill. "How did you know?"

Bill chuckled softly. "You are the only one sitting on a wheelchair while I feel like I was hit by a tow truck, meaning I might have lost something from that impact. I still have to figure out what it is."

Fletcher laughed. "You were always the clever one among the bunch."

Everyone burst out laughing.

They chatted a bit with him, then left the ward, each thankful of the goodness of God for Bill's recovery.

EPILOGUE.

Innu walked with a slight sway to her hips and tilted her head higher, feeling like she could handle everything that came her way. A few whistles here and there and she giggled.

The doctor was discharging Bill today. She had left Reign with his great grandmother and grandfather. Her high heeled shoes tapped on the tiled floor as she walked to the ward.

"I can walk on my own," Bill growled at the nurse on duty while he stood up from the bed.

"You are an impossible patient Mr. Lewis, you know that," Nurse Helga retorted. "Glad I will not be seeing you again."

Innu giggled at the easy banter going between the two of them. She was in awe. He always managed to amaze her over how he made women feel comfortable around him, including the old women falling in love with his charm. Like Jane Cooper, who gathered everyone staying in the building when she heard about the accident, and they offered prayers for Bill's successful operation and quick recovery.

"You're ready to go."

Bill looked up at her when she got into the ward. When he caught a glimpse of what she was wearing, he sat on the wheelchair he had been declining a while ago.

"Good grief woman. What in the hell are you putting on? You want to give me a heart attack."

Nurse Helga laughed and nodded to Innu. "He is all yours."

Innu stretched her leg and turned around after Helga left. She knew she looked great, and his blood had already rushed to his head. A mischievous look crossed her eyes. "What, you mean this little old thing."

"Nurse Helga, bring me a sheet please to cover her immodesty," Bill hollered. Innu winked at him.

She had put on her metallic dress. Aggy had been a darling and mended the sleeves that were torn up that night.

"Don't act like you didn't ogle my legs that night to the point you married me."

Bill laughed, and then froze. "Married."

Innu scoffed. She pulled out the paper that has always been in his wallet.

"Oh and the obvious," she showed him the ring finger and pointedly stared at the hand with the other part of the ring, which she had slipped back on him after his surgery.

"How could you let me think the worst throughout? I thought I had slept with those four men when you could have cleared this whole misunderstanding, by telling me. Innu baby, we got married. I am your husband and you my wife. Get it. How hard could that have been?"

He snorted, "And have you collapsing and even worse, dying from heart failure. You would faint at the drop of a hat." She huffed and continued like she hadn't heard him. "It would have been a shock, but you know, being the mature person I am, I would have taken it in my stride since it would be bearable to the wild thoughts I was having."

"Darling, if you can forget your superman in an instant but still remember the four weasels," he motioned to his height and built. "Something truly is wrong with you."

She rolled her eyes. "Why did you believe me when I lied about being involved with your father and stayed away from me for those days?"

Bill shook his head and stood up from the wheelchair. He pulled her into his arms and hugged her.

"I never believed any of it. I was just too angry that you believed that hogwash about yourself when I had met the vulnerable girl and married her. Of course mom did tell me of the goons that you sent to threaten Fletcher after that incident over Marg fifteen years ago. She couldn't help but laugh about it, that a teen had put Fletcher in his place."

Innu looked up at him in horror. "It's surprising that we never came across each other because I had told my mom after she narrated the story, that if I ever met you, I will marry you on the spot. Then it will be two people irritating the hell out of Fletcher."

She giggled while tears fell down her face and he wiped them off.

This was still unbelievable to them, including the pitch black tunnel they had gone through in order to be together.

Innu had wondered if what she had gone through had been preparing her for him, this gentle hulk of a man, who saw her with a different set of eyes than the rest. Maybe that's why the instant attraction and love, when they first stared at each other in the bar, as each sensed the vulnerability of the other because they both needed to love and longed to give it to another who will love them wholeheartedly in return.

In the month Bill was recovering in the hospital, Norah confessed to knowing of her secret marriage to Bill. Elle confessed to slipping inside Bill's room when Innu rushed out to receive a call. Bill was fast asleep after their eventful night when Innu left the bed, so he never noticed that he was reaching out to another person in bed and whispered he loved her while Innu stood stunned by the door and all her insecurities rushed in to overwhelm her, in that she had been betrayed once again.

Since she had consumed Bill's spiked drink unknowingly, by the time Dwayne found her dejectedly walking down the street and she instantly fell asleep in his car. She couldn't remember what had happened except for the traces of the drug that were found in her system. Dwayne assumed she had been raped while Norah struck as usual to undermine her.

A lifelong revenge she swore to inflict on Innu when her husband ran off with Innu's mother Adele. What Innu wasn't aware of, is that the general had stepped in to help out Norah because of the children, and their lives had remained separate. Theirs was a marriage of convenience. The general stuck to the deal to protect Dwayne and Jeremy while Norah went against the deal and made Innu suffer.

She confessed to meeting Elle in the ladies restroom and offering to help her out to get Bill, then handed her the pill to put in his drink. None of them ever thought Innu would be the one to drink it and Bill would follow her when she left that place.

When Innu woke up confused, Norah paid four unscrupulous men to pretend they indeed had slept with Innu and once Innu found out she was pregnant, the guilt overwhelmed her. She felt she had betrayed someone but didn't know who it was. When the nightmares started, and the panic attacks, her step mother continued to make her feel worse. The last straw was the painful labor she went through, that nearly killed her and for Norah to inform her, the child never made it.

The child was too weak, fighting for his life when Norah handed him to Elle who contacted Bill for assistance. Bill never realized that Innu was in that same little remote town, fighting for her life, after the complicated birth while his son fought for his life too.

His family was made up of some pretty tough fighters, which he had come to realize after he too woke from the hit and run. The man was apprehended. As it turns out, it was Elle's brother. The trump card Norah always held over her, since she overheard Elle asking her brother and his goons in the club plotting on how they would teach Innu a lesson, while she danced at Bill and was oblivious to all of it. Elle's brother was the same man too, who had approached Innu at the company dinner and she started experiencing the panic attacks after he whispered that he would reveal her secret to everyone. A vicious cycle is what they had been through, orchestrated by a revengeful person.

"Are you ready to go home captain Lewis," she asked after they shared a long passionate kiss.

"And where is that?" He dropped his arm over her shoulder and they walked out of the ward.

"Where else, a place Reign is most familiar with. I can't believe you made that woman stay with him there."

"It's my house Innu, and it will be Reigns in the future." She huffed and stamped his foot. He swore beneath his breath.

"A clueless man is what you are," she retorted and walked ahead while he limped behind.

"How can you still be nice to her after everything she did to us? I couldn't get the smell of her out of that house you know. But I finally did." She finished with a devilish twinkle in her eyes.

"Innu what did you do?"

They were now in the parking lot and she was reaching for the handle to the car. She stared at him and shrugged. "As it turns out, my husband is not a pauper, so a makeover is what I did."

He groaned. "Don't tell me what I think it is that you did."

He got into the car on the passenger side. "If you are thinking that I got rid of everything and bought new furnishings, clothes and toys, then you are absolutely correct."

Bill's jaw dropped. He looked ahead, holding his temper in check. She really was so vindictive. When she fought back, the impact she always left was bigger, since she would pretend to be hopeless where finances were concerned. Her father had warned him about this before he added, *Please be firm with her, or you will be bringing her back to me in no time.*

"Mhm Innu."

She continued to drive and briefly looked at him before her eyes went back to the road ahead. "Yes love."

"Am I allowed to call you out over the temporary clause? You did say if I ever got tired of you, I could end it. I'm already tired."

She smiled. "Nope. You had your chance buster and decided *permanent* worked for you. So I am now a permanent girl. Besides, do you think I am like that generous bimbo of yours who could settle for pieces of you?"

"Elle is not my bimbo."

She huffed. "I did see you pick her up over your shoulder on my birthday. I was so jealous and pissed off with you, since I was on my way to tell Dwayne that his dare had backfired. I had been knocked down by a bulldozer and I wanted to make crazy love to that outrageous flirt and make him realize that I was the only one for him."

Bill groaned. Elle was a nuisance that day. She plastered herself on him after Innu's parting remark over her boyfriend and he had been infuriated by both women, Innu for being so clueless while Elle tried so hard. He had picked Elle up and gone with her to the ladies restroom before he shut the door in her face and commanded her to wash her face and sober up.

By the time he went back to the bar and Elle appeared to be in her senses, she handed him the drink as a peace offering. He saw Innu and he approached her. She had seemed stunned like something had shocked her and all he had wanted to do was protect her from the pain. Innu blankly looked at him then grabbed his glass and gulped the contents down.

Elle came again, all scratchy cat and yelling on why Innu had taken Bill's drink. Who was she to him? Bill was hers.

Innu sadly smiled and walked away, while Bill was left to take Elle to the room before he looked for Innu and he found her in that alley.

He froze over what she had said. She had decided to break up with Dwayne! "You remember." He asked in disbelief.

She rolled her eyes. "Bits and pieces, here and there. The heartache, all because of you mister. Not bloody Dwayne."

"Oh sweetie."

"Don't touch me. I am driving. Do you want us to be involved in an accident?"

Bill chuckled and shook his head. "Of course not. Why would we have an accident when my touch does nothing to your insides?"

She threw back her head and laughed in disbelief and glared at him.

"Bill Lewis, how could you? You used the seduction technique you Fletcher's are rumored to have on the dance floor? Then you did the same on the balcony when we met. You nearly made me think I was going crazy when I craved your touch in all those instances."

Bill feigned being shocked. "Darling, I would never do that on an unsuspecting person. The massage is a myth perpetuated by our womanizing father."

She snorted on that, now not believing a word of it. She snapped a finger, while one hand remained on the steering. "You called it putting in a shell. That's what you did to me. Putting me in a cage was more like it, since you ruined my life."

"Did I ruin your life, really?" He gave her that look which said, *woman, can you hear yourself talk.* She giggled.

From the moment they met, she thought she had made him putty in her hands when it was him all along. Damn.

"You Fletcher's are something else," she shook her head in despair. She was ruined. Hell she had been ruined three years back to the point even when on a good day she felt she could be with someone else, another man's touch revolted her nonetheless, and she found herself involuntarily flinching.

"Why did your ancestors pass down the techniques on how to pleasure a woman, of all things? Why not useful stuff like how to restore world peace."

He chuckled. "That's why the harems darling. The many wives. One woman is not enough for a Fletcher."

She pulled over on the dirt road, and then turned to face him. "Now you listen to me buster. One wrong move and your manhood will end up on a platter. I will satisfy your fetishes. No woman, or man," she wiggled her brows, "will be sharing our bed." She finished with a threat in her eyes.

"Not even an inanimate object like a toy."

"No Bill," she shook her head and then did something crazy. Unclasped her seat belt and shifted to him before she gave him the passionate kisses that always left them panting for more. Lucky for them, the path was lined up with trees and was traffic free.

She was all sexy and raunchy as she touched him, nipped on his neck and he gave the same treatment. They were finally going to get it on. Three years of abstinence, gone and done away with, in the car like a bunch of teens and not the married couple that they were.

Bill groaned and nipped at her sweet lips, and then she decided to take a breather when his hand was slipping into her panties as she winked, and easily slid away from his reach, leaving him horny as hell. "For the times you held back on me. I mean how could you be that selfish, when your body now belonged to me actually."

"Innu, you do know, some men have raped their wives after they played at a stunt like this."

She stuck out her tongue. He growled in frustration at the naughty woman he had married.

He sat up, trying to catch his breath from that little interlude and about to make another suggestion that would benefit them both. Didn't the woman understand that as a Fletcher he had insatiable needs and as a man of faith, those needs could only be met by her. His beautiful wife. Hadn't he starved for long enough?

"No Bill," she answered.

"How do you know what I wanted to ask?"

"I know your mind, that's why. You were about to suggest we head into the fields."

He snorted and to his annoyance she started driving. She briefly touched his hand in comfort before she looked ahead. "Trust me sweetie. If we get into those fields, we will never come out of them."

Bill laughed. His wife was such a vixen. They continued in that way, her refuting everything he suggested after, especially at the firmness in her tone. He did succeed in getting what he wanted when they were getting out of the car at their home. When he did touch her the way he knew how and she became putty in his hands.

They never made it to bed and Bill was muddled up to notice the significant changes she had made until he was well sated to even have the strength to be angry with her. It was five hours later and they had gotten a snack. She was right, they would have remained in that field if they had decided on the little detour, considering that short reprieve to the kitchen for a snack as he took in the bold colors of the furniture and walls was just that, short.

Innu giggled and easily slid into his arms before she whispered a few outrageous things they still had to try out. His last note before they made love again was, *you will kill me before my time is up because for some reason you enjoy the havoc you create in my world, not only with my sex life but with everything. You are just too much.*

Where once upon a time, Elle had maintained the bachelor feel for him, a burst of color is what Innu had brought.

Reign came in the next day with his great grandma and grandpa, Dwayne and Mia with their two children, Jeremy with his girlfriend, Bill's mom and brother with his wife and children. Catherine with Ralph and their son Brandon, while Gina surprised Innu when she turned up eight months pregnant with her husband Geoff on the side. She had kept the news from everyone and wanted it to be a surprise. Marg with Garret and their children, including Fletcher who was boasting that he has always known Bill would turn out good.

A happy family is what they had yearned for the most and that prayer appeared to have been granted to them in boundless leaps.

Bill and Innu looked at each other during the meal and smiled. They held their hands and mouthed to each other, *I love you,* before they resumed with the conversation on the table. They had finally set their roots and had what they never would have imagined before. A loving family.

The End

AUTHOR'S NOTE:

Thank you for reading The Temporary husband! This story is the first in the Fletcher series. As promised, I had hinted in 'The Arrangement' that I would work on a couple of novels to feature Margaret and Garret's friends and family.

I hope you enjoy these stories as much as I enjoy writing them. If you enjoyed Bill and Innu's story, I would appreciate it if you would help others enjoy this book, by recommending it to your friends and reviewing it.

BOOKS BY AUTHOR
FAMILY MATTERS SERIES
1. The Inconvenient Marriage
2. Finding a husband for Cissy
3. A Risky Venture
PERFECT GENTLEMEN SERIES
4. The Arrangement
5. The Perfect Gentleman
6. The Designer's Wicked Intentions
NEXT GENERATION SERIES
7. Sweet Crazy Love
8. Loving a Compton
ARRANGED MARRIAGE SERIES
9. The Pastor's Wife
10. The Wrong Couple
ROYALTY SERIES
11. The Prince's Bride
INSPIRATIONAL ROMANCE
12. Leila

FREE SHORT STORIES
13. The Unsolved case
14. His obsession, her hero
THE FLETCHERS
15. The Temporary Husband
ABOUT THE AUTHOR

Yvonne spends her time musing over what love is and how it seems to affect people in their whole outlook to life. She lives in a small Mining town of Hwange with her family. Fans can contact Yvonne on the following sites:

Facebook https://www.facebook.com/vovosibbs

Once in a while, Yvonne drops a cover image of the latest book she would be working on. Information pertaining to promotions to her books can also be found on her Facebook page which you can use to your advantage by clicking on the links provided.

WordPress https://yvonnesbooks.wordpress.com

You can also read some of her work in progress at the above-mentioned site, including short stories she would have written for your enjoyment.

Yvonne is grateful for your support in her writing venture and thanks you all.

To God the Father, Son and the Holy Spirit, may your name be ever glorified. Amen